Mike Faricy

Bulldog

Bulldog

ISBN 13: 978-1508641339

ISBN 10:1508641331

Acknowledgments

I would like to thank the following people for their help & support:

Special thanks to Donna, Rhonda, Julie, Sam and Roy for their hard work, cheerful patience and positive feedback. I would like to thank family and friends for their encouragement and unqualified support. Special thanks to Maggie, Jed, Schatz, Pat, Av, Emily and Pat, for not rolling their eyes, at least when I was there. Most of all, to my wife Teresa, whose belief, support and inspiration has, from day one, never waned.

To Teresa

"I'm knackered"

Bulldog

Chapter One

The first time I saw Dermot Gallagher his right hand held a pint of Mankato Ale and his left arm automatically wrapped around shapely, sexy Casey, the girl who'd come to the bar with me. We were best friends by the end of the night, Dermot and me, me and Casey…well not so much.

Dermot had been in his uniform that night, a black tunic and a saffron kilt. He was a drummer in an Irish bagpipe band here in town. Maybe that was it, the uniform or maybe Casey just had a thing for guys in skirts, I don't know. He turned out to be a really good guy, with a dry sense of humor, sort of quiet, but only because he was taking note of everything going on around him. He had dark hair, wore glasses and stood about six feet tall with a ready smile. He and Casey were married the following year. I was deployed at the time.

The smile was gone today. The mortician did a pretty decent job, but if you knew Dermot like I did, well it just wasn't the same. The white silk lining on the inside of his casket didn't do much to help matters. There was a rosary wrapped around his hands. I never knew him to be particularly religious, hell maybe he wasn't and he was just hedging his bets. That would be just like him, a final, subtle joke on his way out the door. We'd lost guys when I was deployed, even so you never get used to it and that experience certainly didn't make this any easier.

"You about ready, Dev? I guess they're lining up at the door to carry him in," Casey placed a hand on my arm and gently pulled me away from Dermot. It was a couple of minutes before eleven. The visitation in the vestibule of the church had been going for a couple of hours and the church was packed.

Casey was a little thing, maybe five-two, blue eyed with a slight figure. She was dressed in black and proving herself a hell of a lot stronger than me right now. I walked over to where the priest and the other pall bearers were assembled and waited quietly.

The undertaker rolled Dermot's wooden coffin up to the doors going into the chapel then directed us in a soft voice. "Line up here, lads, three to a side. We'll raise him up then arms on the shoulder of the man across from you. No rush, we'll walk at a modest pace to the front and you'll set him on the stand before the altar. All right now, everyone ready?" he asked.

A couple of guys nodded, I guess I was still too numb. We took hold of the brass handles and hoisted the coffin up to shoulder height, rested it on our arms stretched to the man's shoulder across from us then after a nod from the undertaker we stepped off. At least three of us had been in the service which put everyone more or less in step. Not that Dermot was particularly heavy, it was just I don't know, I can't remember really. I was okay for the first few steps, then the organ started playing and I came close to losing it. A clearing of the throat and a hard swallow got me back in line.

We carried him up the aisle, then back out at the end of the service an hour later.

I don't remember much, Casey and her extended family walked behind us. Casey carried a large, framed photograph of Dermot giving everyone a last look, tears were running down her cheeks and she was biting her lip, but she made it.

We carried Dermot to the hearse and after the short drive to the cemetery, from the hearse to the grave site. Dermot's band was there, twenty some folks standing in formation playing Amazing Grace on the bagpipes while we carried him to his final resting place. God, and I thought the church had been tough. The moment I heard that tune, the tears started running down *my* cheeks.

And then it was over.

<u>Chapter Two</u>

We were back at The Spot for a farewell toast and a bite to eat. It was crowded and there was a lot of false bravado being shouted back and forth. Casey was nursing a Jameson with a brother on either side for support. She came from a tight family and they would make sure she was okay. Folks kept coming up to give her a hug and pay their respects. I don't think she ever got the chance to take a first sip.

"Get you a beer?"

I turned around to see my pal, Aaron LaZelle a lieutenant in St. Paul's homicide department. Detective Norris Manning was behind him and gave me a polite nod.

"Thanks, but no thanks. If I start today I may not stop."

"You gonna be okay?" He sounded like he really meant it. Manning had turned away and was eyeing the assembled crowd.

"Yeah, I'm fine this is just a tough one."

"They're all senseless, but this one, Jesus," Aaron said and shook his head.

"Any idea, any leads."

He shook his head again, then said, "Nothing of any consequence at this point, but we're not about to give up."

Of course what else could he say? "You need anything from me you just give the word," I said.

"Actually, what we need is you not getting involved. I know how you feel, believe me we've both been there." Manning turned and nodded agreement then went back to scanning the crowd.

I saw no point in commenting.

"You let us do our job and we'll get whoever did this, Dev. I promise."

"Just for the record, the guy had no enemies. He wouldn't hurt a fly, same with his wife, Casey. They're just good folks."

It was Aaron's turn to nod. "That's what we heard over and over, just the nicest folks."

"Still the same story?" I asked. "He just answered the door and some bastard shot him?"

"It seems to look that way at this point. I'd say the wife's scream from upstairs frightened off whoever was there. It's just not making a lot of sense at this stage, but then does it ever? Like I said, we'll get whoever is responsible."

I was going to say something like '*I hope you get them before I do,*' but a little voice inside my head said '*Shut up, stupid,*' and for once, I listened. Looking back, I think that was probably the first inkling that I wasn't going to wait. If I'm yelling, my temper might be on the loose for a moment, but I quickly get it back in check. It's when I'm quiet or soft-spoken that I'm probably the most dangerous. I can become cold, very unforgiving, and I'm capable of some horrible things. I'd been that way from the moment I learned someone murdered my friend, Dermot.

"Anyone seem out of place, here?" Aaron asked. Manning was still scanning the crowd.

I shook my head. "Most of these folks I know. Like I said, everyone loved the guy. It just doesn't make any sense and I'm not buying the random option."

"It's possible, but the chances of it ever being random are pretty slight. There's always the off chance some loon is in the crowd here getting high on people's reactions or the sense of tragedy. You know, suddenly they think they're important because they caused all this," Aaron said.

"Jesus."

"Yeah. Well I think we'll be going. I'm not going to pay my respects. It's always a bit disingenuous and just seems to add more stress to an already stressful situation."

I nodded then said, "I meant it. You need anything on this you let me know."

"We'll do that, Dev. You let us handle it. I know it doesn't seem like we're moving fast enough, but give us some time, promise?"

"Yeah, sure."

"Counting on you, Dev," Aaron said then he and Manning sort of faded into the crowd and out the door.

"Was that the police you were talking to earlier?" Casey asked maybe an hour later. The crowd had begun to thin out, but I still didn't think she'd ever had the chance to sip her drink. She'd set the thing down a while ago and apparently lost track of it.

"Yeah, I've known the one guy, the lieutenant since we were kids. The other guy is a detective, I've dealt with him in the past." I saw no point in mentioning Manning had me fingered as the root of all crime, major and not so major, committed in the city.

"What did they want?"

"Just checking on things, they like to make sure everything is as good as can be expected for you," I lied.

"Oh, that's kind of sweet."

"Yeah, that's them."

"Hey, my brother's and some friends are coming back to the house after this, it would be nice if you could join us," she said.

"Thanks."

"No pressure, it's going to be laid back. Hope you can make it." She turned around when a woman tapped her on the shoulder to express her regrets and say how truly sorry she was. Poor Casey was on about hour six of listening to the same well-intentioned comments, which in itself would be exhausting.

Chapter Three

"No, she seems pretty set on selling the place,"
Dennis said. He was one of Casey's brothers. Another
brother, Tommy was reaching into the refrigerator and
passing beers our way. We were in Casey's kitchen,
nibbling from a dozen different plates of hors
d'oeuvres.

"God, they just got the place," I said.

"Well yeah, more like two years now, but what a
mess, it's almost a hundred and twenty-five-years old
and right now there isn't a room that's not torn up. God
bless the two of them, but finishing a project wasn't
their strong suit. Jesus, talk about stars in your eyes,"
Tommy said, then gave a quick glance around the
room.

There wasn't a door hung on any of the kitchen
cabinets. Sections of plywood painted black served as
the temporary counter tops. One of the exterior walls
had been opened up and yellow fiberglass insulation
was wedged between the studs and covered with a
plastic vapor barrier. The ceiling had been gutted down
to the joists and you could see the cloth covered copper
wire from about 1915 running through holes in the true

dimension timber. Next to the wires, the pipe from the 1890 gas light ran to the middle of the room.

"We got some guys coming in to do some sheetrocking and taping, we hope to be painting after that."

"What about an electrician and a plumber, is this joint even up to code?" I asked.

"They're starting Monday, sheetrockers will have to work around them, but we need to get this place on the market. We wait much longer and we might as well wait until next spring. Christ, not much moves in real estate between November and March in Minnesota."

"Is she gonna stay here, I mean while the work is being done?" I asked.

Tommy shook his head. "My two girls are down in Madison at college, we got extra space. She can be as private as she wants or needs to be, she's staying with us until she gets resettled, there's no rush. She was just uncomfortable staying here, no surprise, so she's been with us the last couple of nights."

"How's she doing?"

"Like anyone would, I guess. She's in the bedroom a lot of the time. Comes out and you can tell she's been crying, her eyes are red and puffy, she's sniffling. What can you do except give her a big hug and tell her you love her. Of course then that just starts her up again. I can hear her up in the middle of the night walking the floor. It's gonna take some time."

"So, Casey said you're a PI?" Dennis said then took a sip from his beer and shot a quick glance toward his brother.

"Yeah, I am, but I mostly work on stuff like resumes to employers and things. You know, just making sure job applications are correct and some dork hasn't listed himself as the president of Lehman

Brothers when in fact he's out there delivering newspapers or something."

"So you wouldn't investigate something like this, Dermot's murder?"

"No," I said then took a deep breath in preparation to give the company line. "In an investigation like this, the best thing, the most helpful thing we can all do, is stay out of the way. Give any and all information, even the most remote, seemingly unimportant fact, just give it to the cops. They're equipped to deal with these things. They'll process DNA samples, ask questions, interview folks. They don't need any of us out there screwing things up, and they especially don't need me making a mess of their investigation."

"Sounds like you've already backed off without even taking a look," Dennis said.

"Denny, come on, man," Tommy said.

"No, it's okay, he's right, that is what it sounds like, but I do this for a living, and I have for some time. I know for a fact whatever I do, won't help. Whatever any of us do, unless it's passing on information, is just going to muddy the water and at best slow down the job the cops have to do. At worst it could quite possibly screw things up to the point where they don't catch the bastard. I don't want that on my conscience. I want to see whoever is responsible get nailed."

"You any good at taping sheetrock?" Dennis asked changing the subject.

"No, but I can paint ceilings and walls. You get that sheetrock up, you call me and I'll help you get this place on the market."

"Deal, you need another beer?" Tommy said and opened the refrigerator.

"No thanks, fellas, I got some things I have to get accomplished today. I better find Casey and say my goodbyes. Here," I said and pulled a business card out of my wallet. "Give me a call and I'll help you paint this place."

"Thanks, we'll do that. Nice to meet you, Dev," Tommy said.

"Thanks," Dennis called as I headed for the front of the house.

"You dipshit, what did you say that shit for?" Tommy said as I left the room. I walked beyond earshot and never heard the reply.

__Chapter Four__

It was a couple of nights later. I was in The Spot sitting with Louie talking about everything and nothing. I share an office with Louie, and he pretends to be my attorney from time to time. Actually he's a pretty good guy and has gotten me out of more than a couple of jams. It was obvious, and I appreciated the fact, that Louie had steered away from any mention of Dermot or Casey Gallagher.

"Mike, maybe just one more round," Louie said, then waved his index finger in a sort of circle to signal the same again.

"You clowns said that about two hours ago, and you're still here."

"Lucky you," Louie said.

My phone rang, I could only hope it was Heidi in need of some of my *special* attention.

"Haskell Investigations."

"Dev?"

"You got me."

"Dev, it's Casey. Hey, sorry to bother you, but I'm at the house packing some things up and this car has been going around the block, slowing down in front of the house, then going through the alley checking the back of the house. It's really freaking me out."

"Did you call the cops, call 911?"

"Yeah, but they didn't seem too impressed. They said they'd send a squad car over, but it wasn't a high priority. Something about concert traffic downtown and stuff. It's just really freakin' me out and, oh shit, there he is again. It's this sinister looking black thing, I don't know maybe I'm just losing it. No answer at either one of my brothers so I'm calling you."

"You just stay there, make sure your doors are locked and stay away from the windows. Okay?"

"Oh, God, I'm sorry to be such a pain."

"It's not a problem, we're on our way. You just stay put we're maybe five minutes out."

"Thanks, Dev."

I hung up the phone and said, "Come on, I gotta go to Casey's"

"I just ordered a round," Louie said.

"Mike, hang onto those drinks, we'll be back for them," I said then pulled Louie off his stool and out the door. My Saturn Ion was parked almost in front. "Get in the back seat," I called to Louie as I hurried around the side.

"What?"

"That passenger side door isn't fixed yet so it's tied shut."

"Tied shut?"

"Just get in," I said and slid behind the wheel. The starter groaned and cranked for a long moment then fired up just as Louie got in. I pulled away from the curb before he had the door closed.

"Jesus Christ, what is this, NASCAR?"

"Better buckle up," I said and floored the thing down Victoria heading for 35E.

"You're gonna get stopped," Louie said from the back seat and I heard his seat belt click.

"They try and stop me, they can just follow me to Casey's, too busy with a concert to see what's going on, God."

We made it to the 35E entrance in record time, the entrance ramp is up a slight incline and the speed limit on this section of interstate through town is posted at just forty-five miles per hour. I screeched around the corner onto the entrance ramp then accelerated, we were doing sixty-five and climbing as we shot onto the interstate.

"Dev, come on, another two minutes isn't going to make a difference."

"Hey, some jack-off shot Dermot last week when he opened the door. No one has done a damn thing about it except say how unfortunate it was. Now someone's circling the place and the cops can't be bothered because there's too many folks trying to get to a concert or some bullshit. I'll take my chances speeding, but you better hope whoever is freaking her out has left by the time we get there."

We took the Grand Ave exit off the interstate. The light was red where the exit runs into Ramsey. I slowed just enough to check for oncoming traffic, then ran the light with a left hand turn and stomped on the accelerator heading up Ramsey Hill.

Louie had enough sense not to say anything.

Casey and Dermot's home was on Holly Ave. It's a quiet residential street of Victorian homes built close together. The street is edged with granite curb stones and narrow enough that parking is allowed on only one side. I zipped around the corner onto Holly, then pulled to a stop in front of Casey's place a few seconds later. I grabbed the .38 snub out of the glove compartment. It only held five rounds, but it was all I had at the moment.

I was halfway to the front door, just about to take the front steps two at a time before Louie even opened the car door. There was a picture window in the front of the house with a building permit taped to the glass. A stained glass window in a grape leaf design sat above that. I rang the doorbell, then remembered it didn't work and pounded on the door. It looked like Casey had turned on every light in the house. A high pitched voice answered from behind the door a moment later. "Who is it?"

"Casey, it's Dev, open up."

A lock snapped, the heavy door swung open and Casey stood there wide-eyed. "Oh, God, I'm glad to see you. Thanks for coming," she said then saw the .38 in my hand and her eyes grew wider. "Did you shoot him?"

"I haven't seen anyone yet," I said.

She looked past my shoulder and suddenly gave a long, "Oh…"

I turned to see Louie waddling up the front sidewalk. "It's okay, he's with me. Casey, this is Louie Laufen, Louie, Casey Gallagher."

"Hi," Casey sort of mumbled.

"Nice to meet ya," Louie said sounding out of breath.

"Louie, wait inside with Casey. I'm going to walk around the house, then maybe do a quick drive around the block. Have you seen anyone since we talked?"

Casey shook her head no.

Louie groaned his way up the four front steps. The porch floor creaked with his weight as he walked past me toward Casey and the front door.

"I'll see you two in a couple of minutes," I said and made my way around the back of the house.

I had no idea what I was looking for and there was at least a fifty-fifty chance there wasn't anything *to* look for. Maybe it was just someone looking for an address or a neighbor out for a short drive. Casey had recently been through a traumatic experience and it wasn't that far fetched to say she could be imagining things.

Her garage was locked. All the first floor windows on the house seemed to be secure, the back door was locked. The gate leading out to the alley was closed, an expensive gas grill was still on the deck and the umbrella was still in the glass-topped picnic table. Things appeared to be pretty much in order.

__Chapter Five__

__"I'm sorry I acted__ like such a baby," Casey said.

Louie and I were sipping Jameson in her den. Casey was nursing a cup of chamomile tea. The room had ten-foot ceilings and wide molding painted white around the windows and sliding panel doors. The fire place had a white marble mantel with a large gilt mirror on the wall above it. Green-glazed Victorian fireplace tiles rested in three cardboard boxes on the granite hearth. Casey caught me staring at the tiles.

"They were loose and some had fallen off so we pulled them all off when we had the chimney relined. We were going to reset them this winter, or maybe the next," she said absently.

"Describe this car to me that was driving around," I said.

"Well, I saw it out the upstairs window. I'm bringing more clothes back to Tommy's, so I was upstairs in the master bedroom packing them," she said then nodded toward a half dozen boxes stacked near the front door. "At first I didn't pay any attention, but then probably the third time I saw it drive by it frightened me. It's was dark blue or black, probably black, kinda low slung like and it's all black, even the wheels and the rims. It was evil looking and like I said, it just freaked me out."

"And it slowed down in front of your house?" I asked.

"Yeah, more than slowed down it almost came to a complete stop like it was looking for something, I don't know maybe checking out our address. Then it would go around the block. I don't know why, but after a bunch of times I went into the back bedroom upstairs. I left the light off and a moment later there he was doing the same thing at the back of the house, just sort of sat there looking at the place, then it slowly drove off. Maybe five minutes later the thing was back out there in front of the house." She nodded out toward the street. "Whoever it was, they were definitely checking this place out. That's when I went around and turned on all the lights. I wanted them to think this place was really crowded like we were having a party or something."

"You're thinking of selling this, right?" I asked.

"There's no thinking about it. I just want to be rid of it. I can't stand to…" her voice trailed off and she sat there with her eyes tearing up biting her lip and trying not to cry.

I waited a long moment before I spoke.

"Maybe it was someone who heard you were going to put this on the market and was just driving past to check it out."

"Maybe, but I haven't even talked with a realtor yet."

That slimmed down the possibility, but I said, "Yeah, but I knew and maybe a couple other folks. Could be one of your brothers mentioned it and someone was just taking a look."

"Could be it was someone who was just curious," Louie said. "I think the address was in the news, you know, after…."

"It just really made me feel uncomfortable. What if they come back when I'm not here and do something like burn the place down? After what's happened, I mean they could do anything, right?"

"I think that's highly unlikely," Louie said.

"After what's already happened, this town is full of crazies. God, that's all I need is some idiot burning the house down. I just can't seem to catch a break."

"Tell you what, how about if we help you load that stuff in the car," I nodded toward the boxes stacked by the front door. "Then you give Louie a ride back to his car and if it will make you feel any better, I'll stay here."

"Oh, you don't have to do that, Dev." But she said it in a way that wasn't leaving me very much wiggle room.

"Not a problem, it would be my pleasure."

"You sure? I mean, maybe I'm just being neurotic or something."

"No, in fact the more I think about it, the more I think it's a good idea. I want to do it, please."

"You're sure?" she said and sort of shrugged her shoulders

"Yeah, I insist, come on, let's get you loaded up."

"Okay," and suddenly Casey was on her feet and all smiles.

Damn it.

Chapter Six

On her way out the door Casey had told me to help myself to anything I could find. I was on my second beer with a bowl of chicken wings and some sort of dip and fancy crackers left over from Dermot's funeral. I had everything spread out on the coffee table. The Big Lebowski was playing on the flat screen and I was stretched out on the leather couch. The movie was just at the point where the Dude was in the bath tub smoking a joint while listening to whale sounds, when I heard something toward the back of the house.

Once Casey and Louie finally left I'd gone through the house and turned off most of the lights. I was flaked out on the couch in the den where I planned to sleep and just had a table lamp on for light. I heard the noise again, put the movie on pause, grabbed the .38 and walked out of the den, through the dining room and into the kitchen. There was a small room off the back of the kitchen that served as the laundry room, but the back door was actually off a small porch on the side of the kitchen.

I stood there in the dark leaning against the kitchen sink waiting and looking at the wall across the room. I moved my eyes back and forth between two windows across from where I stood. The windows were maybe six feet apart and about five feet tall. From the outside of the house a person could stand on the little porch where the windows were and really not be seen.

I heard the noise at almost the same time I saw the shadowy figure. The individual was kind of tall and looked fairly broad. I slowly approached holding the .38 out in front of me in a two-handed grip with the thing aimed at his head.

As I moved closer, the face came into focus and I actually recognized the idiot. The flattened nose, the Mohawk hairstyle, a half dozen piercings in each eyebrow and the three rings in his bottom lip left little doubt. Then, there was the gauging in his earlobes the size of a giant doughnut hole. I didn't so much know him as I knew of him. Freddy Zimmerman, Fat Freddy. A wanna be criminal of dubious reputation. I was pretty sure he was a general disappointment to folks on both sides of the law.

Last I heard, Freddy had been trying to win favor with local crime boss Tubby Gustafson by following Tubby around in an attempt to offer *'additional protection'*. That sort of went down the drain when Freddy rear ended Tubby's Mercedes at a stoplight and Tubby's morally impaired enforcer, a jerk named Bulldog, jumped out of the vehicle and made the adjustments that resulted in Freddy's dinner plate nose. I was tempted to shoot, but it would be a waste of a bullet, and then there was the outside chance it would just bounce off his thick skull anyway.

Instead, I flicked on the porch light and watched as Freddy jumped then dropped whatever tool he was using in his worthless attempt to force the window open. He waddled off the back porch and out into the alley toward his car. The 'sinister' looking black Chevy Camaro Casey had described.

Freddy had cleverly left the car almost directly under the alley light. It appeared to be running with the headlights still on. I watched as he beat his hasty retreat out the back gate, past the trash bins and into the alley.

I walked out the front door, climbed into my Saturn Ion and prayed it would start. I drove up the block and rounded the corner as Fat Freddy peeled out of the alley and took off. I followed Freddy at a distance although I had a pretty good idea where he was headed. Along the way I wondered where a numbskull like Freddy got the sort of cash it would take to purchase that Camaro, provided it was indeed purchased and not 'obtained'.

Sure enough, about five minutes later, he pulled into the parking lot of a dive bar named Ozzie's. I waited about thirty seconds and pulled in after him. I sat in my Saturn for a few minutes then went in the back door and spotted him alone at the bar. It wasn't that surprising, who'd want to spend time with Freddy? He was a moron and besides, there were just two other drinkers in the place. They were nursing beers, appeared to be regulars and didn't look up when I walked in giving the distinct impression they would like to just be left alone.

Freddy looked like his usual idiot self. He glanced in my direction and then attempted to hide his face as I came through the back door. His back was to me and he seemed to be studying the front door, maybe calculating if he could waddle out that way and make it to his Camaro before I caught up with him.

The bartender slid a bottle of beer in front of him and then stood there waiting for payment. Eventually he raised both hands, palms up and sort of wiggled his fingers in a *'Come on, man, pay up'* motion.

"I'll get it, and give me a pint of Mankato Ale," I said then tossed a ten on the bar. The bartender grabbed the ten and nodded, then gave Freddy a strange look. He was back with my beer a minute later. I tossed a five on the bar and he looked at me. "Keep it, I'd like to be private with this gentleman for a moment."

"Suit yourself," he said sounding like I'd made a really bad choice, then rapped the bar a couple of times with his knuckles to acknowledge the tip before he moved to the far end.

Freddy grabbed his beer and took a healthy sip keeping his back to me.

I stuck my little finger in his ear gauge and pulled.

"Ouch, hey what the…God you're killing me, stop it, stop it, dude. Christ, you're gonna rip my ear, bitch."

"Then look at me, Freddy. Where the hell are your manners? How you been?" I said and pulled my finger out of his ear. His voice had a nasally tone which I guessed came from the nose adjustment Bulldog had given him after rear ending Tubby Gustafson's Mercedes.

"Oh, it's you," he said rubbing his ear lobe and shaking his head. "You're that dick guy, right?"

"Private Investigator," I corrected.

"Yeah, that's what I meant, man. Ahhh, thanks for the beer."

"Not a problem, Freddy. So tell me, what have you been up to?"

"Up to? Me? Nothing really."

"Gee, that's funny. See, I was just taking it easy over at a friend's house and all of sudden I hear a noise. Guess what?"

Freddy looked nervous, reached for the beer bottle and drained about half the thing.

"Come on, Freddy, take a guess."

"I ain't got any idea, Mr. Hassle, honest."

"It's Haskell, fuckwit. So, guess who I saw trying to get into my friend's house? Guess who was trying to break in?"

"Oh, I wasn't trying to break in. He just wanted me to see if there was a way to get in there, that's all. I…" All of a sudden he shut up as if it dawned on him he'd already said too much.

"Trying to find a way in? Into *my* friend's house? For who?" I asked then pulled the .38 out of my pocket and shoved it in my waistband making sure Freddy could see my every move.

"I probably shouldn't have said that. I didn't really mean it," he said, sounding even more nervous.

"Hmmm-mmm, does that mean *you* were going to break into *my* friend's house?"

"No, no honest."

"That's good. I didn't think you'd do that, Freddy. At least I hope you wouldn't, because that would make me very mad and I'm sure neither one of us would want that, would we?"

"No, you're right, that wouldn't be good."

"Yeah, right, so who were you checking things out for? Who's trying to get into *my* friend's house?"

"I really can't say."

"Yeah you can, Freddy. You can tell me, after all we're pals. Look, I even bought you a beer."

"Yeah, I know, I already said thanks and all, but I really can't tell you."

"Sure you can, Freddy, well unless you want to see that fancy car of yours out there in the lot maybe get torched and then after I set it on fire, I'm gonna come back in here and look for you."

"Me?"

"Yeah, and I won't be happy, because you're playing me for a sucker and that makes me mad, Freddy. It really does."

"I'm not playing you for a sucker, Mr. Haskell, honest. It's just that he can be kind of mean and all and…."

I stuck my little finger back into Freddy's ear gauge and pulled.

"Ahhh-hhhh, God don't, come on that really hurts. Don't ahhh-hhhh."

"You got about three seconds to tell me, Freddy, or I'm going to rip this thing right out of your ear."

For just a brief moment the bartender looked over from where he was sitting at the far end of the bar watching the ball game, then he went back to watching the TV.

"Three, two…."

"I can't, I can't tell you they'll…."

"One," I half yelled and yanked the gauge out of Freddy's ear.

"Ahhh-hhhh," he screamed loud enough that one of the regulars looked down our way and the bartender stood up off his stool and said, "Take it outside, fellas," in a loud voice.

I grabbed Freddy by the back of the neck and moved him toward the front door.

Freddy had a bloodied hand over his ear and was screaming, "You maniac, are you fucking crazy? God, you tore my damn ear off, what in the hell is wrong with you? Jesus, that hurts."

"Listen to me, you fat assed idiot, I'm gonna tear that gauge off your other ear, give you a matching pair unless you tell me what you were doing trying to get into that house tonight. You think I'm fooling? So help me God you better start talking or I will tear you apart."

"I already told you, I can't, he'll kill me."

"That's exactly what I plan on doing," I said and reached for his other ear.

Freddy pushed me away and started to run for his car. I sort of half jogged and caught up then dropped a foot or two behind while he kept waddling, trying to fish his keys out to unlock the car door. The lights on his Camaro blinked a moment later as he scurried toward the driver's door. He pulled the door open and just as his fat ass was halfway in the car I slammed into the door full force.

It banged against Freddy and he gave a high-pitched yelp then staggered back a step or two. There was a vertical crease along the outside of the door where I slammed into it. I grabbed him by his Mohawk and bounced his head against the doorframe a couple of times. He stumbled back and started to slide down the side of the car. I lifted him with an uppercut to the chin and heard his teeth clack, then drilled him in what was left of his nose.

"Okay, okay, stop it, God. It was Bulldog, Tubby's guy. Okay, you happy? Jesus, lay off, bitch, I didn't do anything to you. God!"

"Bulldog?"

Freddy was bending over at the waist leaning against the Camaro with his hands on his knees. Blood from his nose and mouth was dripping down into a puddle on the asphalt parking lot. Blood from his ear had soaked a good portion of his shoulder and the front of his shirt. He stared at the ground and didn't look up at me when he spoke.

"Yeah, Bulldog. He didn't tell me why, honest he didn't. He just said he wanted to get into the house, that the folks were moving and he was thinking of buying it back. Wanted to see what they'd done before he came up with a number."

"Buy it back?"

"Yeah, that's what he said, honest," Freddy gasped.

"Why didn't he just call? That doesn't make any sense," I half said to myself, but Freddy heard me.

"I don't know, man. It's Bulldog, it's not supposed to make sense. He just told me to go there and find a way in. He said no one was living there. If I knew your friend was there I wouldn't have tried the window, really, I wouldn't lie to you. I promise I wouldn't," Freddy said then coughed and spit more blood a couple of times onto the asphalt.

Chapter Seven

I was lying awake on the couch at Casey's
wondering why Bulldog wanted to get into this place.
It's not like there was anything to really steal, maybe
the flat screen, but a jerk like Bulldog would have
access to an entire truckload just by making a phone
call. Dermot's laptop was three or four years old and
besides, I didn't think Bulldog knew the alphabet. Then
there was the bit that he, Bulldog was a previous owner.
Knowing Dermot and Casey, they would have run the
other way rather than deal with someone like him. I
double checked to make sure the .38 was on the coffee
table then promised myself I'd call Casey in the
morning and drifted off to sleep.

"Rise and shine, Sleeping Beauty," Casey called
and set down a couple of bags and a tray holding four
coffees.

I sort of groaned then rolled over and sat up. My
shoulders, neck and back made audible cracking sounds
as I twisted left and right, then I burped.

"Charming. God, you slob, how could you trash
this place all by yourself in just one night?" she asked
then placed my ice cream dish in the bowl full of
chicken wing bones. She stacked the empty dip

container on top and picked it all up along with the cracker box. "I'll come back and get all the beer bottles and I better bring the vacuum, you've got crumbs all over. There are toothbrushes in the top drawer to the right of the bathroom sink. Might be a good idea, then come on back, if I remember correctly you like caramel rolls for breakfast."

"I like anything I don't have to cook," I said. Then picked up the .38 as discreetly as possible and slipped it into my pocket.

We were sitting in the den. Two plumbers were banging pipes out in the front room doing something to the radiator. I was almost finished with my second coffee and eyeing the third. Casey was about halfway through her first and still nibbling at the same caramel roll she'd started on twenty minutes earlier. She was doing the female thing; taking the smallest of bites, barely a morsel, eating that and then waiting. I'd already inhaled both my caramel rolls and was picking up errant crumbs from off the coffee table. I eyed the rest of her's and decided to play rough.

"God, I guess I should have gotten more," she said watching me lick my finger tips.

"Nah, this was great. Really hits the spot. I have to say, Casey, you look really great, have you've lost a little weight?"

"Probably just the stress."

"Well, you look like you've been working out, you look fantastic."

"Thanks, Dev, that's sweet," she said then pushed her plate to the center of the coffee table. "Go ahead and finish that if you want, I'm really not that hungry."

"Nah, I couldn't. You sure, I mean you barely touched it?"

"Please, take it otherwise it will just go to waste."

"Okay, I guess if you really don't want it," I said moving the plate over into my domain.

"No really, I'm full."

"Hey, mind if I ask you something?" I said then took a bite that cut her caramel roll in half.

"Ask me and we'll see."

"I was wondering, how long have you guys been in this house?"

"You mean like why isn't it finished?"

"No, I didn't mean it like that."

There was a sort of window bay area maybe five feet deep on the exterior wall of the den with four tall windows. The roof had leaked and probably still did where the bay jutted out from the main structure. Casey glanced up at the water-damaged plaster on the ceiling. It was cracked and stained a yellow brownish color. Unfortunate past experience told me those stains would bleed right through any paint. But then the plaster was so damaged the area would have to be replaced anyway so it didn't really matter.

"All my friends from the burbs were always asking us when we were going to be finished. They just don't get it, but then how could they? Anyway, let's see, it was May when we moved in, and we had to get the furnace replaced before we moved. I think we closed the end of March. So that's…" She counted silently on her fingers, then said, "So I guess that's about twenty-eight months."

"You remember who you bought it from?"

She ignored my question and took a detour down memory lane instead. "It was going to be our house forever. I mean with four bedrooms upstairs there'd be plenty of room for kids. We were going to live here for the next fifty years. Of course things happen and…"

"Do you remember who you bought it from?" I asked again. "Who lived here before you?"

"The seller?"

"Yeah, was it a family or an old couple, who was it?"

"I can't really say. It was sort of strange. It was never officially on the market, you know with a sign out front or anything like that. We sort of heard about it by word of mouth, I can't even remember who told us. I do know it had been empty, but not for too long. Sort of a weirdo character at the closing representing the sellers. He was a lawyer I think, Johnny or Jamie something. I suppose I've got his card around here somewhere in a file, sleazy type, with a home dye-job on his dreadful slicked back hair. He kept leering at me and I remember when he gave me his card he sort of held my hand and raised his eyebrows like there was a lot more available if I wanted it."

"What did you do?"

"Ran to the ladies room and washed my hands with disinfectant, twice. What a creep."

"We never met the owners, I think they were traveling or something?"

"Traveling, like they were in the circus or what?"

"Yeah, that's right, Dev, the circus. No, it was like they were out of town, out of state for that matter. I don't know Europe, Hawaii, China maybe, anyway not living the sort of life we had," she said and then I could see the tears beginning to well up in her eyes and so I changed the subject.

"Hey, how would you feel if I moved in, temporarily, just so the place isn't empty at night?"

"Did you see him, did he come back?"

"No nothing," I lied. "I would guess it was someone like Louie said. You know, they heard this might be going on the market and they wanted to drive by. That might actually be kind of a good thing since you're going to sell."

"Yeah, I won't be able to keep up the payments by myself and then, well probably not the best idea to stay. Hey, I appreciate the offer, Dev, but I really can't impose on you like that. After all, you were kind enough to come last night when I phoned in panic mode and…."

"Casey, it wouldn't be an imposition. Really, besides you'll sleep better and you know how I can worry so how 'bout we just agree I'll spend the nights here."

"I could pay you, not much, but…."

"No. You don't need to pay me. I'd like to do it, really."

"You're sure?"

"Yup."

"I mean I could probably…."

"No, Casey, look I'll be back here around five tonight. If you could go out today, maybe get me a set of keys, we'll be all set."

"I suppose you could use Dermot's," she said and then the tears welled up again.

Chapter Eight

"You're kidding me, the two you are shacking up?" Louie asked.

"No, you low dripper, we're not shacking up. She's staying at her brother's place. I'm just going to be there at night to make sure no one breaks in."

"Did you tell her about that Fat Ass guy?"

"Fat Freddy? No, to answer your question. Nothing I could say was going to help in that vein, God she'd just obsess and worry. I just told her it had been a quiet night and let it go at that."

Louie nodded.

"I could use your help on something."

"What's that?" Louie asked.

"Well, if you wouldn't mind doing a little research, maybe you could sort of check out the history of the place. Fat Freddy said they bought the place from Bulldog. Casey said whoever owned it was out of town traveling in Europe or China when they closed on it. That sure doesn't sound like Bulldog. I'm going to wander over there this afternoon, knock on some doors to introduce myself and see if the neighbors can tell me anything."

"I'll check it out. When you talk to Casey, ask her if she has a copy of the abstract, it might be interesting to go through that."

I nodded, then said, "She mentioned some sleazy lawyer handled their closing. Guy actually made a pass at her. His name was Johnny or Jamie something like that, he had slicked back dyed hair. Ring any bells?"

"Sleazy, God it could be just about anyone. Jackie Van Dorn comes to mind. He's certainly sleazy. He's got this pencil thin mustache thing and dyed black hair, God knows why, the only person he's fooling is himself. Looks like something out of a 'B' grade movie from the 40's. Yeah, I could see him making a pass at someone during a real estate closing. He fancies himself as a man-about-town, it's comical."

I was knocking on neighbors' doors later that afternoon. No one answered at the two homes on either side of Casey's place. The third house was a three-story, two-toned green Victorian that sat directly across the street. I climbed the steps to the front porch and knocked on the carved oak door. A large picture window looked out onto the porch, a stained-glass window in a floral pattern sat above it.

"Yes," a voice called from behind the door.

"Hi, I just wanted to introduce myself, my name is Dev Haskell. I'm going to be spending some nights across the street at Casey and Dermot's."

A nice looking woman opened the door a moment later. I pegged her around mid-seventies and thought I may have recognized her from Dermot's funeral the other day.

"Hi, my name is Dev Haskell," I said again.

She opened the door wider and gave me a top to bottom examination, visibly moving her head up and down. "Are you a policeman?"

"No, I'm not. I'm just a friend of Casey and Dermot's. Under the circumstances, Casey is a bit uncomfortable spending evenings there and so she's staying somewhere else. We just didn't want the place to be empty at night, with all the publicity it seemed like it might be inviting a problem. I just wanted to say 'hi' so when you see some strange guy wandering around over there, well, it's me."

"Mmm-hmm, dreadful business that was. We've all been on guard ever since. Who would have thought? The taxes we pay in this city and that sort of thing happens, I don't know. Oh, now just listen to me going on, how is she doing, Casey?"

"I think pretty well under the circumstances. She's here every day, hauling some things out, clothes mostly, and then checking in on the workmen. There were plumbers there this morning and I think a contactor, kind of tough to keep up."

"So sad, I can't blame her for not wanting to stay there, but we so loved her. Loved them both, such a pity. They'll be missed," she said and shook her head.

"Do you know who lived there before? Who they bought the home from? I have this feeling I was here once before, a few years back, but it's not ringing any bells. I just can't seem to put my finger on it."

"Well, yes and no. There were a host of renters through there over the better part of five or six years until Casey and Dermot moved in. Good lord it became the worst home on the block, all sorts of awful characters coming and going at all hours of the day and night. God only knows the sort of nonsense that went on over there."

"Then the Gallagher's bought it, thank God. But as to who owned it, who they bought it from, no I don't actually know. We've been here forty-six years, the

Speer family was in there for a good twenty plus then someone bought the home from them and immediately turned it into a rental property. Things seemed to go downhill quickly from there. You can just imagine."

"There was one woman, strange sort of thing. Unbalanced might be the best word I can think of. Dressed like she was the worst sort of street person, but I heard from one of the neighbors she was some kind of missionary."

"Missionary?"

"Yes, apparently she was involved in a kind of preaching and saving souls or some such business. I suppose if you're going to be saving those afflicted it helps to look and act like them." She raised her eyebrows in a way that suggested there might be a lot more to the story then she knew.

"You don't remember her name?"

"No, I haven't the foggiest. To tell the truth, even if I'd known she was saving souls I'd still keep a safe distance. You know how it goes, trouble just naturally seems to find that sort."

I guess I did know, maybe. I thanked her, gave her my card and left. I couldn't put my finger on it, but there was something she said that seemed to ring a distant bell. My memory was hazy at best and it was like looking into a thick patch of fog when I tried to come up with whatever or whoever it was. I went back across the street, sat on the porch swing and waited for Casey.

Chapter Nine

Casey showed up a little after five and gave me a wave as she climbed out of her car. She looked both ways before she crossed the street then chirped the car alarm system and headed toward me.

"Hope you haven't been waiting long."

"No, not at all, plus it's been about a thousand years since I sat on a porch swing."

"Really?" she said and climbed the steps.

"Yeah, I think the last time I was on one of these things I was sitting on my mom's lap."

"Oh, so like two or three years ago…"

"Yeah, right. To tell you the truth, I'd forgotten how really nice it can be."

"Wow, looks like you're moving in to stay," she said looking at my suitcase by the front door.

"Just some extra clothes so I don't have to be running back and forth every day." I didn't think there was any point in telling Casey I had two more pistols, a pair of binoculars and close to a hundred rounds of ammunition packed in there with my boxers.

"Feel free to use the washer and dryer, they're almost brand new," she said then caught herself for just a brief moment. It was over almost before it began, but you could sense the heartbreak.

I moved on. "Hey, Louie wondered if you could get hold of the abstract for this place. He wanted to study it for a bit, look at the history of the house. He's actually a lawyer."

"He is?" she said sounding more than a little surprised then said, "You know I think you already told me that. It's just with everything that's been going on I'm sort of a little spacey."

"Not a problem."

"Here, at least I remembered to get a set of keys made for you," she said and handed me a white plastic bag with 'Ace Hardware' written across it in red letters. "Maybe try them in the lock and make sure they work."

I inserted the key in the front door lock, turned it and heard the lock click.

"Wow, lucky guess. The other one is for the back door and then that different looking square kinda one is for the garage. Dermot's car is in there and the garage door opener is probably still hanging on his sun visor. You might as well park in my space I'm not going to be using it."

"I'll check it out," I said.

"I'm just gonna grab a couple of things and then get over to my brother's. You need anything before I go?"

"No, I'm just fine, Casey, don't worry."

"I really appreciate you doing this for me, Dev. You know deep down you really are a good guy."

"God, don't tell anyone."

She smiled at that. I helped carry three loads of boxes to her car, then about a hundred different tops on hangers, a bunch of shoes and a suitcase that was so heavy she must have packed it full of books then sat on the damn thing just to get it closed. She lowered her window once she started the car. There was just enough room for her to sit in the driver's seat. Stuff was piled in the backseat up to the rear window. The passenger seat was loaded up almost to above the dashboard.

"Don't make any fast right hand turns because all that stuff will just tumble down on top of you," I half joked.

"Thanks again, Dev, I really appreciate it. Stay safe," she said and drove off.

I went inside and unpacked. I just piled my clothes on one of the chairs in front of the fireplace in the den. I had a snub .38 in my pocket and I stuck a Walther PPK in the small of my back. Then I grabbed a beer and another tray of left over hors d'oeuvres and retreated to the flat screen. I watched some movie with a title I couldn't recall. It had a car chase scene and some numbskull able to dodge bullets from an AK on full squirt at a distance of about ten feet, that's Hollywood for you.

I was thinking about Casey. Pity we never really connected when we were dating. I put her on my list of good women who somehow got away then decided that another beer and some of those cookies out on the kitchen counter couldn't hurt.

Chapter Ten

It was just before lunch when Louie washed up on shore at the office the following morning. I was standing at the window with my binoculars watching one of the girls on the third floor of the apartment across the street. She was ironing something in just a thong and bra. Her back was to the window and she seemed to be watching the television on her kitchen counter while she worked.

"You checking license tabs on the street making sure everyone is current?" Louie asked then tossed a computer bag on his picnic table desk.

"Something like that, I'd feel bad if they weren't up to date."

"Any coffee left?"

"Should be, I made some this morning."

"How'd it go at your new place last night?"

"You mean Casey's? Fine, no problem except that she's got work crews coming in there in the morning, a couple of plumbers, some contractor. Man, those guys are out front by about seven-thirty in the damn morning."

"There's a seven-thirty in the morning, too?" Louie said then settled into his office chair and blew on his steaming coffee mug.

"Pretty tough talk for the guy who shows up just before lunch."

"I've been in court all morning. There must have been a push to nail guys driving while over the limit last February or March. I pled three DUI's this morning."

"Humpf, probably St Patrick's Day. Any luck on getting the charge reduced?" The subject of my attention on the third floor across the street had moved into one of her other rooms and unfortunately reappeared a minute or two later dressed. I set the binoculars back on the window sill and sat down behind my desk.

"In today's world it's just plain luck that no one will be serving time, first offense for all three, but the days of getting it pled down to a simple speeding or failure to signal are long gone."

"That's probably good. I mean we've all been behind the wheel when we shouldn't have been."

"When did you become so politically correct? You're right, but each one of these guys, it's gonna run them about ten grand by the time they pay the fine, have their driving privileges restricted for six months, pay court costs, my fee and then increased insurance rates for the next seven years. Two of these guys are married, you can just imagine the fallout on that front."

"No thanks."

"Hey, Jackie Van Dorn. You mentioned him yesterday, hitting on your friend Casey at her real estate closing."

"Yeah, the sleazy lawyer?"

"Right, I got an update this morning in the hallway outside the courtroom. If he was representing the seller and when did you say this happened, a couple of years ago?"

"Yeah, Casey thought it was maybe twenty-eight months, almost two and a half years ago."

"Well, the word I got is your pal Jackie has been exclusive for at least four or five years just handling transactions for, get this, Big Boy Enterprises."

"Big Boy? You mean Tubby Gustafson?"

"Yup," Louie said then put his feet up on the picnic table and took a sip of coffee.

Tubby Gustafson was our very own homegrown mobster. I'd run into some unpleasantness with him in the past and felt the best way to avoid any future problem was to just stay away, actually make that as *far away* as possible.

What Louie said made sense in an unfortunate way; Jackie handled Tubby's business, Bulldog was in Tubby's employ. Suddenly it sounded like Fast Freddy really was telling the truth the other night. If sleaze ball Jackie Van Dorn did in fact handle the closing with Casey and Dermot then there was a good chance that psychotic moron, Bulldog really had been the seller. Of course, that led to the big question, why did Bulldog want to get back into the place? Especially after almost two-and–a-half years.

"…it for quite some time. Anyway, the things you find out just chatting in the hallway," Louie said then sipped some more coffee.

I tuned back into the present. "So does that mean Tubby or Big Boy Enterprises owned the place or was this just sleazy Jackie being a nice guy for a change and attempting to help poor old Bulldog out?"

"I suppose it all depends, I'm having a tough time seeing Jackie helping out and being nice to anyone."

"I chatted with a neighbor lady across the street yesterday. She told me the place had been rented for five or six years before Casey and Dermot bought it. That it went steadily downhill with all sorts of sleazy bullshit going on there day and night."

"She say who owned it?"

"No, she didn't know. Of course it isn't a far leap to see Tubby or Bulldog getting hold of a piece of real estate and turning it into an absolute dump. This woman referred to it as the worst house on the block before Casey and Dermot bought it. I'm guessing someone was running drugs or maybe women out of there. God, they were probably cooking meth in the basement."

"Brings up a lot of questions about Dermot's murder," Louie said.

"Yeah. There's that, and what Fat Freddy told me about Bulldog the other night, that he was just casing the place for that Neanderthal. I still can't figure out why," I said.

"Just a guess, this is far fetched, maybe, but do you think they have bodies buried in there, maybe beneath the basement floor or something."

"Oh, God, I hope not. Casey doesn't need something like that happening just before she puts the thing on the market."

"Plus, I mean it's a city code violation," Louie said.

I looked over at Louie.

"Just kidding, relax. I mean it is…."

"I know that, Louie, but I don't think that's it. The guy is going to essentially sneak into the house and what, dig up a body or bodies plural and sneak them back out of the house? That's nuts."

"Look who we're dealing with here, Dev."

"There is that, but I still don't see it. Why not just knock on the door and ask to come in or pretend to be a city code inspector or something and you're just there to inspect. It's too simple not to pull something like that, the work crew isn't gonna question you coming in. The home owner isn't around during the day."

Louie shook his head. "Something else is going on, Dev. God only knows what."

"I think I might pay a visit to your close, personal friend, Mr. Jackie Van Dorn."

"Man, hang onto your wallet and any gold you have in your teeth."

"You know where his office is?" I asked.

"I know where it used to be, far as I know he still offices there, you'll love it."

"Where's he at?" I said then pulled a pen out of my desk drawer to write down the address.

"Last I heard he was still above Nasty's.'

"You're kidding?"

"Actually, if he's now exclusive with Tubby it sort of makes perfect sense."

Chapter Eleven

Nasty's is a local institution featuring over-priced drinks, crabby bartenders and naked women. It has a six-foot red neon heart over the door with the word *'Nasty's'* scrolled across the front flashing on and off. The last time I was in there I'd been told to leave in no uncertain terms by one of the bouncers. Okay, I was kicked out, but not for being abusive or, abusive in my usual way. I'd been on a case and attempted to ask one of the dancers some questions. She took offense when I didn't want to pay her, made a scene and I thought the best thing I could do was comply with the wishes of the gentleman who looked like he pumped weights all day and wore a T-shirt advertising the Ultimate Fight Club Boot Camp. I hadn't been back since.

I'd never met Jackie Van Dorn, but I agreed with Louie that in a strange way it seemed fitting he would office here. I went through the front door into a small entry room that housed a heavy-set woman stuffed behind bullet proof glass. The little area she was in was so small her arm and shoulder were pushed up against the glass and I immediately thought of a large sausage stuffed into a very small jar. She laid the romance book she was reading face down next to her smoldering cigarette and coughed out, "Five dollars."

I hated cover charges. I half wondered what kind of attorney would charge you just to get into his office then realized how really stupid that sounded. I slipped the five bucks into the little well in the counter and she slid a 4x5 color brochure back to me advertising a sex toy shop. She took a drag from her cigarette, didn't bother to look up and went back to reading her romance.

The entry to the bar area was just past the ticket booth, a semblance of music thumped out from behind a pair of double doors. The large brass handles on the doors were in the shape of a pair of boobs, which seemed sort of fitting. I automatically raised my hands and pushed through both doors.

Not much had changed inside Nasty's since the last time I'd been kicked out, except it looked a little more rundown. As my eyes adjusted to the dim lighting, I noticed the place had the definite reek of cheap perfume and dumb guys. The floor was covered from the double doors all the way up to the stage area in leopard skin carpeting with a red boarder running along the walls, and looked like it hadn't been cleaned in years. The fifteen-foot stage was lit by colored flashing lights with a mirrored disco ball slowly spinning from the center of the ceiling. The back wall of the stage was all mirrors and a chrome pole was positioned on either end of the stage.

It was late afternoon and maybe just a half dozen bored patrons sat by themselves at different tables. Two guys sat up along the stage with maybe four empty stools between them and a pile of one-dollar bills stacked up next to their drinks. A couple of dancers wandered across the floor wearing negligees, sipping watered down drinks and offering lap dances. No one was buying.

The woman grinding her back up and down on one of the chrome poles had a look plastered on her face like she'd just passed out with her eyes open. I made my way to the bar.

"Yeah?" was the less than cheery greeting I got from the bartender. I would have pegged her age at about fifty, but given the lifestyle she was probably closer to thirty-five. I'd obviously interrupted whatever daydream she'd been involved in.

"Actually, nothing for me, I'm looking for Jackie Van Dorn's office. I think he's up on the second floor."

"Yeah, he is," she said then stared back at me, bored.

"How do I get up there?" I said looking around in a way that suggested I couldn't find the door.

"You go outside around to the back of the building it's the door next to the dumpster."

"Back of the building?"

"Next to the dumpster," she replied.

"Gee, thanks."

She didn't smile, nod, or give me the finger. She just walked down to the far end, leaned against the back of the bar and pasted the same blank look on her face as the woman swirling around on the pole. On the way out I didn't waste my time asking for my five bucks back.

There were actually two dumpsters in the back of the building, one green and one blue. If they were color coded for some purpose it would appear no one had bothered to pay any attention. Both of them smelled equally bad.

The metal door at the back of the building was painted navy blue enamel, red primer showed through were the paint had chipped off the door. A small metal sign was fixed to the door that read 'Sentinel Security.' Someone had penned the word *'Sucks'* behind Sentinel Security. There was a doorbell in the grimy metal doorframe and a security camera mounted overhead on the wall. The door was locked so I pushed the doorbell and heard a long buzz echo from somewhere inside.

A moment later a voice came out of a speaker in the camera mounted overhead and said, "Yeah?"

"Hi," I said giving my nicest smile as I looked up into the camera. "I'm here to see Mr. Van Dorn."

"Got an appointment?" the voice growled.

"No, I'm sorry I don't. I wasn't sure how to get in touch with him."

"What's it about?"

"I'd like to take that up with Mr. Van Dorn."

"Your name?"

"Haskell, Devlin Haskell."

I heard the speaker click off and I waited, still smiling for the camera. A moment later there was a loud click and a buzzer sounded, I turned the doorknob then pushed the door open. There was a steep staircase about three feet inside the door with no stair rail and a dim yellow light about a mile away at the top of the steps. The cinderblock walls on either side of the stairwell were shiny with the same navy blue paint that was on the door, I started to climb.

At the top of the stairs was another metal door, this one was open and I stepped through into a short hallway with a room maybe ten feet ahead. I could feel the music from below vibrating through the floor and the smell of cigarette smoke grew stronger as I approached.

The room was paneled in the sort of wood paneling that had been popular in basements during the 60's. A woman sat at a large wooden desk in the middle of the room half hidden behind a computer screen and a smoldering cigarette. There was a beige push button phone circa 1980 sitting on her desk off to the left with four clear plastic buttons at the base, signifying land lines. One of the buttons was lit.

"He's on the phone, just take a seat," she said not looking up from her computer screen. I could see the reflection in her bifocals of the solitaire game she was playing on the computer. Behind her was a closed door. I took a seat in one of the plastic chairs against the wall and waited.

After a good fifteen minutes, the beige phone buzzed and without looking up she said, "Guess you can go in now."

"Thanks," I said and headed toward the closed door.

Louie's description of Jackie Van Dorn as a 'B' grade movie star from the 40's wasn't far off the mark. He sat behind a massive desk and sized me up as I entered his office. From a good fifteen feet away I could spot the home dye job on his black hair along with maybe a quarter inch of grey roots showing, all of it slicked back and fitted to his head like a helmet. His mustache looked like it had been drawn above his thin lip with a cheap eyebrow pencil. He wore a light blue shirt with a starched white collar and a fire engine red tie. His coat was snow white with a red pocket silk that matched his tie. I pegged him for about a hundred years old. He studied me from behind a pile of files as I approached.

"Mr. Van Dorn, I appreciate you making time to see me without an appointment," I said and extended my hand.

He looked at my hand for a moment and then, probably against his better judgment gave me a limp shake in response.

"Mind if I sit down?" I asked.

"Be my guest," he said almost under his breath. The way he continued to stare gave me the feeling he was trying to read my mind.

"So," I said taking a seat in an uncomfortable green leather chair and waited. Then I waited some more. I could feel the vibration from the music down below in Nasty's throbbing through the floor. Finally I broke the ice. "Your name came up regarding a real estate deal from a couple of years back and I wondered if you might be able to help me."

"I guess that all depends." His massive black leather chair squeaked as he tilted back and appeared ready to listen. The red lining of his suit coat became exposed and appeared to match his tie and pocket silk.

"A friend of mine was involved in a real estate closing about two-and-a-half years ago. You represented the selling party. I guess they were traveling or something. Anyway, I wondered if you might be able to provide some information on them, the sellers."

"Information? What sort of information?" he asked then stroked his chin with his hand.

"Well, their name for starters."

"That's a matter of public record I'm sure you could get in touch with the county and they could tell her."

I didn't know if the 'her' was a guess, a slip of the tongue or was he just letting me know he knew exactly why I was there.

"Along with their names I wanted to find out something, actually anything I could learn about them."

"I don't intend to reveal my client's name just from the confidentiality standpoint, I assume you understand. Frankly, if you want the name that bad you can look it up. As far as *finding out* about them I really couldn't be of much help. Without going into specifics, my only dealings would be related to that particular transaction, hardly the sort of interaction that would allow me to gather information and then pass that on to you. There is that troubling little item called ethics that comes into play."

"Ethic's" I said and nodded. "You've a bit of a unique practice, Mr. Van Dorn, don't you more or less keep Tubby's feet away from the fire."

"I wouldn't really know what you're referring to Mr. Haskell and I think I've been more than generous with my time. Please enjoy the rest of your day," he said then pressed a button on his desk. A moment later a rather large individual entered the office. He showed the residual effects of a beating, a purple discoloration across the bridge of his flat nose and beneath both eyes, although the swelling had all but disappeared. His lip was split on the right side and seemed to be healing somewhat slowly. His entire right ear was bandaged up in white gauze. His eyes grew wide as I turned in the chair to face him and a sadistic look of recognition splashed across his face. He reached behind his back and pulled out a rather large looking .45. Fat Freddy.

"I'd like you to see our guest to the door. He's finished here," Jackie Van Dorn said, then sort of shooed me away with a few flicks of his hand.

Fat Freddy waved the .45 at me indicating I was going to leave. I wasn't about to argue, I rose to my feet, gave Freddy a wide berth and headed for the door. "Thank you for your time, Mr. Van Dorn, I'm sure we'll be in touch," I called over my shoulder.

Van Dorn didn't respond. The woman at the desk didn't bother to look up from her solitaire game which one could only hope she was losing. I walked out of the room, down the short hall then picked up speed once I was at the top of the stairs.

"Oh no you don't, not so fast," Fat Freddy said under his breath then hurried down the steps after me.

I had to slow down to let him catch up. He thundered down the steps grunting. His hand holding the .45 was placed against the wall for balance. He was busy focusing on the stairs when I half turned, reached up and grabbed him by the wrist then twisted him over my shoulder. I hung onto his wrist and yanked the .45 out of his hand as he let out a loud groan then slid down a half dozen steps. His head bounced off the wall a couple of times and he skidded to a stop at the bottom.

"Freddy, Freddy, Freddy, you just don't seem to learn," I said then stepped over him, opened the door and walked outside. Freddy remained where he was, sprawled across the steps coughing and groaning. For my part, I couldn't see any benefit in hanging around, so I quickly made it to my car and fled Nasty's.

Chapter Twelve

"Yeah, I didn't think you'd get anything out of Van Dorn," Louie said then twirled his index finger at Jimmy to signal another round. We'd been in The Spot for a couple of hours.

"What a sleaze ball."

"Told ya," Louie said.

"Did you know the entrance to his office is next to a couple of dumpsters behind Nasty's?"

"No, I didn't, but it's not all that surprising, in fact it's almost poetic now that I think about it."

"I put a call into Casey about her abstract hopefully she can get hold of the thing."

"Yeah, like I said it would be interesting to look through it. You get the name of the seller it's probably nothing, but it just might be a good idea to pass that information on to the police," Louie said making it sound like a pretty strong suggestion.

"Yeah, I know, I know," I groaned.

"You worried about this Freddy character? It doesn't really sound like you've gotten the relationship off on the best foot."

"There is no relationship, Louie. I want that idiot and anyone else who may be associated with him to just stay the hell away from Casey and from me."

"I get that, but just be careful so you're not inviting more involvement on their part."

Some guy walked in the front door and I glanced outside, it wasn't quite dusk, but it would be dark in less than an hour. "I better get a move on, I want to be at Casey's before it gets too late and have some lights turned on. You want to stop over for some week old chicken wings and beer?"

Louie seemed to ponder my offer for a brief moment then shook his head. "No, it would probably be the better idea to just head home."

"Of course it would, but since when have you ever done that?"

"True, but I'll still take a rain check."

"Suit yourself, man. See you tomorrow."

Louie nodded then signaled Jimmy for another drink. I went out to my car and headed toward Casey's. There was a pair of headlights behind me as I drove down Victoria toward the entrance ramp, nothing unusual, I just made a mental note. They followed me onto the interstate which was still okay. I took the next exit, Grand Avenue and they followed. That was a little unusual, but it's happened before. When I took a left up Ramsey then turned left a block later onto Grand instead of going up Ramsey Hill, it started to feel a little weird. I was on a city street and the headlights were hanging back, but I was pretty sure they were following me.

By now it was too dark to see what type of vehicle it was. My money was on a 'sinister looking' black Camaro with a crease in the driver's side door where

I'd jumped against it to bounce the thing off Fat Freddy the other night.

I took another right, drove a block and hooked right again. It had to be Freddy, who else would do such a horseshit job of tailing someone? I drove the rest of the way to Casey's house with one eye on the rearview mirror. When I turned onto Holly Avenue the headlights behind me kept going straight down Arundel. It looked like a black Camaro in my rearview mirror, but I couldn't be positive. Maybe Freddy just wanted to see where I was going and then head home. Maybe, but I doubted it.

He was going to do something stupid, I just knew it. I parked across the street from Casey's, went in the house and turned on a number of lights then ducked out the back door and waited next to a hedge along the side fence. From where I stood I could see the back door and the front yard.

I didn't have to wait long, Freddy came hobbling down the street about fifteen minutes later. The gauze bandage on his ear was like a headlight in the night. He cut through the next door neighbor's yard and headed toward the back of the house. I moved toward the back and stepped in close to a large lilac bush. Freddy rattled the side gate then slipped into the backyard. I watched as he peered into a back window then tried to sneak along the side of the house passing no more than ten feet from me. He cautiously crept up the steps to the deck then glanced around. He didn't seem to be carrying anything, at least not in his hands, so I figured he wasn't going to do something stupid like toss a bomb through the window. Still, it was a safe bet he was armed.

I let him take a couple of steps across the deck before I called out. "That's far enough, Freddy. Stretch your arms out where I can see them and don't move. You do anything stupid and I'll shoot you."

He stood still and spread his arms out wide. He hung his head like he couldn't believe he'd already failed at this undertaking, too. I came up on the deck behind him, pushed the barrel of the .38 into the back of his head just so he'd get the message then patted him down.

When I pulled a pistol out of his waistband he let out a frustrated sigh, sounding amazed I'd found it in the most logical place.

"Freddy, just what the hell is it with you? Honest to God, haven't you had enough? This just doesn't seem to be working for you."

"I told you before, I'm doing this for Bulldog."

"Doing what? So far you've been beat up, thrown down a set of stairs. Your nose has been broken, you're limping and you got that ear thing going for you. How's it been working up to now?"

"Well, not so good to tell you the truth, you didn't have to be so rough the other night at Ozzie's and you could have really hurt me on those steps this afternoon, God, I'm all black and blue and…"

"Freddy, you ever think of taking up a different line of work?"

"You kidding? I'm a criminal and I'm pretty good at it. It's kind of like we're in the same business. You know?"

"Not really."

"Hey, Haskell can I put my arms down, I'm getting kind of tired standing like this and my back is killing me from those damn steps this afternoon."

"Yeah, sure, Freddy, look you want a beer? Let's talk and see if we can't help each other out."

Chapter Thirteen

We were sitting at the kitchen counter halfway through our second round of beers. Once I took the clip out of Freddy's pistol and checked the chamber for a round, I gave it back to him.

"Yeah, thanks it's the only one I got left," he said then glanced at me like that was somehow my fault.

"So what were you doing at Jackie Van Dorn's today? Are you working for him or bouncing at Nasty's?"

"I guess Bulldog thought it would be kinda funny to have me be a bouncer at Nasty's. To tell you the truth, it gets pretty boring. Everyone thinks it sounds really cool, but it isn't. Most of the girls there are okay, but they aren't really interested in me. The other bouncers, I think Bulldog told them to give me a hard time, he's kind of a prick to tell you the truth."

"No surprise there."

"Anyway, it doesn't really start to get busy until a little after five so I'm the only guy bouncing there in the afternoon. Bulldog called my cell this afternoon and yelled at me to get my ass upstairs to Van Dorn's office. I guess he was the one who called Bulldog and told him you were up there."

"Van Dorn called Bulldog?"

"Yeah, least that's what I was told. But he must have, 'cause Bulldog was out making collections at the time so he wasn't even there."

"Collections?"

"Yeah, it's a pretty neat deal. A bunch of places pay Bulldog to kind of watch their business, you know so they don't get robbed and stuff."

"A protection racket?"

"I don't know about that," Freddy said looking completely oblivious. "He just makes sure no one hassles them. You know?"

"And what happens if they don't pay?"

"I don't know, I don't think that ever happens."

"How'd you like to make a hundred bucks, Freddy?"

"Maybe. What do I gotta do?" he sounded very cautious.

"I'd just like to have you take me around, see what the businesses are. You know, get some ideas for myself."

"See what the businesses are? They ain't fancy, they're just little joints."

"I'd still like to see them, and its a hundred bucks."

"Would we have to go inside?"

"No, just drive by, in fact if you want we could take my car. It blends in, no one would know you're even there."

"I don't think Bulldog would be too happy about that if he found out."

"So don't tell him. Hundred bucks, Freddy just driving around for maybe an hour tops. It's not like I'm gonna go in and talk to the people and I'm certainly not gonna tell Bulldog. I could pick you up, or better yet, we could just meet somewhere, early tomorrow morning. Get it done before anyone is even out of bed."

"I 'spose."

"How about this, you know where my office is, right?"

Freddy nodded.

"You park on the next street over. Anyone sees your car you can just say you were watching me. I'll drive you around, you can point out the places. All we'll do is just drive past."

"Think maybe I should wear a disguise?" Freddy asked sort of warming to my offer.

"If you want to do that, think it would help, sure, go ahead."

He nodded and suddenly looked excited.

We finished our beers and Freddy left by the back door. He went back out the side gate, limped through the neighbor's yard and then up the block. I tossed the clip from his pistol into a kitchen drawer.

Chapter Fourteen

I was parked on the side street next to my office reading the paper in my car while I waited for Freddy. He was already twenty minutes late and I was beginning to worry he had blown off our get together and wouldn't show.

I spotted him in my rear view mirror, limping down the street toward my car. The gauze over his ear was covered up by what looked like a five dollar black wig hanging down to his shoulders. I set the newspaper down to cover the .38 resting on my lap then watched him approach. Despite our little conversation and sharing a couple of beers last night, I didn't trust the guy any further than I could throw him.

He knocked on the passenger window then opened the door and climbed in. "What do you think?" he asked then raised his eyes toward the top of his head to indicate the cheap wig. It looked like it was nylon or rayon or something, you could see an elastic band running across his forehead and there were a number of wispy strands statically clinging to his face. He blew air up toward his forehead in an effort to move the strands, but it only served to make more of them attach to his face.

"I think it's perfect, and it covers your ear, good thinking."

He smiled at that.

"You carrying, Freddy?" I asked.

"Well, yeah sort of."

"Sort of?" I said.

"I got my pistol, but you took the clip last night and I don't have another, so it ain't really loaded."

"Here's that hundred bucks, maybe go and get yourself a new clip." I said and handed him five crisp twenties.

"Actually, I was thinking of getting two and they're like sixty bucks apiece," he said then nodded and looked hopeful.

I ignored his price quote and said, "Let's get a move on, where's the first place?"

It turned out they were all over on the East side of town, a total of sixteen different commercial businesses, just little storefront, mom and pop type of operations. There were three places that did nails, a grungy coffee shop, a diner sort of joint, two convenience stores and a little hardware store. On and on it went, most of the businesses had bilingual signs posted in the front window, some in Spanish, some Asian, and one or two looked to be African.

The pattern was developing, people maybe not all that familiar with laws and rights we take for granted. Coming from societies where this sort of intimidation may have been the norm.

As he pointed out the various locations Freddy would make an off-handed comment regarding the payments. "That's a hundred bucks, one-fifty there, those folks pony up close to two hundred a week."

Over all, doing a rough calculation I figured the little protection racket brought in close to three grand a week, round it up to a hundred-and-fifty-grand a year paid out just to keep Bulldog from wrecking the place. And that was just the places Fat Freddy knew about. It wasn't that big of a leap of faith to think a jerk like Bulldog would start out every day strong-arming people.

"And this all goes to Tubby?"

"Tubby? I don't know anything about that. I've just been with Bulldog. 'Course these are just the places I've been to, I'm sure they got more, maybe lots more," he said that like it was a given, after all everyone did it, didn't they?

"So back up a minute, Freddy. Bulldog never mentioned Tubby?"

"Hunh?"

"I asked you if all that money went to Tubby and you said you didn't know."

"I guess I never thought about it like that. Bulldog kinda pockets some cash, maybe, sometimes, then puts the rest in this black leather case he carries." Freddy looked out the passenger window and sort of squirmed

"He takes some cash?"

"Well, maybe he skims a little off the top, I guess, kind of."

"Think Tubby knows?"

"I don't think so and no one is dumb enough to tell him."

"Why not?"

"You kidding? First of all he wouldn't believe it and even if he did, he would probably go right to Bulldog and ask him. Of course, Bulldog would say no and then he'd be wise someone told on him and then that guy would be dead."

It sounded like a pretty black and white operating structure; 'Tell the boss and I'll kill you,' simple as that.

"What if Tubby did believe, what if you had proof?"

"Proof? Like what? A video or something? That wouldn't cut it and anyway by the time Tubby was convinced, well, Bulldog would have already killed you so it still wouldn't work. It just seems to work out best if I shut up. The last thing I need is that big prick Bulldog riding my ass more than he already is."

"He's pretty tough on you?"

"Let's just say he doesn't make it very easy and leave it at that."

I wasn't sure what, but I could sense the germ of an idea just beginning to percolate.

Chapter Fifteen

It was the fourth night I'd been sleeping at
Casey's, and great as it was, I was beginning to get
tired of my own company. I called Maureen to see if
she'd like to come over and eat what was left of
Dermot's funeral food.

"Hello," she always sort of drew that word out in a
sexy sort of way, saying 'Hell-lo' like she was singing.
It sounded happy, positive, up beat, and indicative of
good things to come.

"Hi, Maureen, Dev Haskell."

"I told you, I don't want you calling me."

"What?"

"You heard me. What part of *'don't ever call me
again'* don't you understand?"

"I thought you were kidding. I mean come on, it
wasn't that big a deal, was it, really?"

"Yeah, Dev, it was to me. Not showing up for my
Mother's birthday, telling me you had to work out of
town."

"I was out of town."

"Yeah, that's right, you were, shacked up with
some floozy if I recall."

"That might be a little harsh, I…"

"Hey, Dev, listen to this," she said and hung up.

I called Karen and left a message. She sent a text message back that said she was blocking my number. I was losing interest fast so I phoned Heidi.

"Hi, Heidi."

"Stop right there, if you are calling with a problem, need a ride or bail money, Do. Not. Even. Ask. Because I'm going to hang up."

"Gee, nice way to start out. Are we having a bad day?"

"No, at least not up to this point. I'm just telling you, Dev, so don't go there."

"All right, apparently that's what I get for wanting to ask you out. I guess I'll just entertain myself if that's the way you're going to be."

"You don't want anything?"

"Maybe just a kiss and a hug, I sort of thought being in your company might be a nice way to spend the evening. God, sorry, my mistake."

"Okay, okay, it's just, well you know the last couple of times we've been together you always had an ulterior motive."

"You can't blame me for being attracted, Heidi. God, sorry I happen to think you're beautiful and sexy."

"Thanks, that's sweet, but that's not what I'm talking about. There was the bail I had to post last winter. The ride I had to give you when your car broke down."

"That wasn't my fault, those guys set my car on fire."

"Yeah, and then I had to drive ninety miles to go get you and bring you back. Then the time you left me in the car when you got arrested and I ended up having to call a friend."

"Because you took a selfie with the cop looking in the car window then laughed about it. He got really pissed off and I'm the guy who got hauled in."

"Yeah and left me there in the middle of the night with no way to get home."

"So are we going to go through every little mistake I've made or would you like to go out? I've got something you might like."

"I'm not doing tequila shots again."

"Not that, look remember my friends Dermot and Casey?"

"The guy who was murdered?"

"Yeah, I'm staying in their home, I just thought you might like to see it, you're sort of into all that decorating stuff and it's an 1890's Victorian place. A lot of fancy woodwork, stained glass, antiques and that kind of junk. I figured you might find it interesting. They've got all sorts of shit."

"God, all sorts of shit, how could I resist?"

"You know what I mean."

"I think so. What time?"

"You name it, I'll pick up dinner and if you want I'll pick you up, too."

"I'll drive myself, Dev, that way I can ditch you when I get fed up."

"What do feel like eating?"

"Chinese and pick up Dim Sum, too."

"You got it." I gave her the address, then I gave her very specific directions. Heidi's really smart, but she was hiding behind the door when they were passing out a sense of direction. She's lived in St. Paul all her life and she can still get lost going to a friend's house. However, she does make up for it in other ways.

Chapter Sixteen

Heidi arrived in style, Heidi style, forty-five minutes late. Not that it mattered, I planned on giving her a short tour of the house, we'd wolf down the takeout dinner, then get down to the real business, my immediate needs.

"Oh my God, this place is so cool," she said when I opened the door. Then she brushed past me and wandered into the front parlor. "Oh I love it, and the wood work, the turned spindles. Did you notice the design pattern on the cedar shakes outside on the second floor?"

"What?"

"That figures," she said and just shook her head.

I poured her a glass of wine in the paneled dining room with the sliding doors and built-in breakfront and we proceeded with our tour. From the dining room we went back into the front parlor with the fireplace and the stained-glass windows. We checked out the den where I'd been sleeping on the couch next to the three boxes of glazed fireplace tiles.

"I think it's so cool they're going to reinstall these tiles, they're gorgeous. Don't you think?"

"Yeah sure, whatever."

"God, you are so completely hopeless. All your laundry piled up on that chair and scattered around the floor adds a nice, homey touch. Here, get me another glass of wine and let's check out the second floor."

She spent ten minutes getting up close and personal with the staircase, "Get out of the way, Dev, here hold my wine glass I want to take some more pictures," she said handing me the glass and then shooing me out of the way.

It dawned on me that I'd only been upstairs a couple of times and that was just to carry clothes out to Casey's car. "I think there are four bedrooms up here," I said leading the way. Heidi wandered into the master bedroom, took about a dozen more pictures of that fireplace, then more pictures of the small dressing room next to that.

"Look at this, Dev, you can still see where there was some sort of stove in here for heat that's what that round plate is up on the wall. The chimney's behind that and the stove pipe used to connect right up there."

I nodded, sipped some more beer and said, "Amazing."

Heidi just shook her head like she couldn't believe it. We walked down the hallway, to a back bedroom. Two steps led down into the room.

"This would have been the servants' room, that's probably why the steps are here," she said. The room was smaller, less grand than the other three bedrooms, the ceiling maybe a foot lower. "Yeah, this closet area was probably a staircase down into the kitchen originally. The help could go down there early in the morning, get things going for the family."

"Gee, just like today," I said.

"It was a different time, Dev. If you lived in the area when this was built and didn't have live-in help,

72

you would have been viewed as socially irresponsible, for starters. Oh wow, look at this, the cabinet, kind of a funny place for a built-in. I wonder why they went to the trouble to put that in here."

"Hey, what about some dinner, are you hungry? Looks like you could use some more wine, too."

"Just wait a minute. Look at this cabinet, Dev, it can't be original to the house, it probably was built in the twenties or thirties. It's so cute," she said backing up and taking more pictures with her phone.

"Okay."

"Not okay, it's beautiful, but it's really strange that it's here, in the back of a large closet. I'm sure they pulled out the back staircase. What's below this?" she asked and knocked on the wall around the cabinet, it sounded hollow.

"Below this closet? It's the bathroom off the kitchen, just a sink and toilet, no shower or tub."

She nodded. "Has this always been single family?" she asked then knocked on the wall again.

"No, when Casey and Dermot bought it, the place had been converted to apartments, I don't know how many, I think someone mentioned maybe five or six units. I talked to the woman across the street and she referred to it as the worst house on the block once that happened. I'd say probably not the best clientele living here."

"Well, they've done a wonderful job. There must be a space back there behind this cabinet, certainly not big enough to be a room, it's strange."

"Hey, I'm going to get your dinner going in the microwave, you want to join me or would you rather stay up here in the closet and knock on all the walls."

"I'm coming, oh this has been so cool. Thanks, Dev, you know every once in a while you do something nice."

"Thanks."

"You can be sweet," she said and gave me a peck on the cheek. "You can also get me another wine."

Chapter Seventeen

It was just before seven the following morning when Heidi left. "I've got a conference call at nine and an eleven o'clock meeting," she said then kissed me and let herself out. We'd gone to sleep in front of the flat screen in the den. After sleeping on the thick Oriental rug and using the couch cushions as pillows my body felt like a bent piece of plumbing. I was in my boxers cleaning up the little white takeout food containers and putting the wine bottles in recycling when the workmen showed up.

I arrived in the office and was seated at my desk by nine, unsuccessfully scanning the building across the street with my binoculars. Louie made it in a little after ten.

"Any coffee left?" he asked as he came in the door.

"Fresh pot on, I made plenty for you."

"You sound like you're in a pretty good mood, anything happening over there?"

I put the binoculars down and spun round in my chair to face him. He was wearing his wrinkled gray suit today, as opposed to his wrinkled navy blue, gray herringbone, darker gray, brown or wrinkled black suit.

"I got a text message from Casey this morning, she's going to give me that property abstract tonight so you could go over it tomorrow if you've got time."

"Great, I'll make time I'd like to look at it. I don't have a lot shaking in the morning, at least as it stands now." He had just poured himself a mug of coffee and was walking back to his picnic table desk carrying the mug. As he sat down in his chair, coffee sloshed out of the mug and in one fell swoop got his lapel, his white shirt and his tie. "God, can you believe this crap?"

"Maybe you should have set the mug down first."

"Thanks for that thought."

"Say, I went for a little ride with your friend, Fat Freddy, yesterday."

"My friend," Louie said then licked the back of his tie and attempted to dab the coffee off his shirt. It looked as if he only succeeded in making the stain a little larger. "Damn it."

"Maybe you should just leave well enough alone," I suggested.

"Fat Freddy, you were saying."

"Yeah, we drove around over on the East Side and he showed me a bunch of places Bulldog is providing protection for."

"You two are pals, now?"

"In a way, I sort of feel for the guy. He's just an idiot."

"Well, say no more, there's the common bond."

"Anyway, it's a protection racket, Bulldog and most likely Tubby got going. They're screwing these small business guys. Looked like a lot of immigrant-type places. I'm sure it's folks unfortunately afraid to go to the cops and rightfully afraid of Bulldog."

"What a jerk."

"You think? Near as I can figure out, from just the places Fat Freddy showed me, they're getting close to three grand a week. And like I said, that's just the ones I saw."

"Three grand a week. What is that a couple hundred bucks from each of those places?"

"Yeah."

"Every week? God, that's probably their entire profit margin."

"Certainly could be. Freddy alluded to Bulldog skimming some off the top. Man, I'd like to nail that creep."

"Stay away, Dev. Nothing good can come from you getting involved."

"I'm not going to get involved, I'd just like to nail him is all."

Louie just shook his head, took a sip of his coffee and opened a file. I put the binoculars back up and returned to my unsuccessful scanning of the building across the street.

A text came through from Casey around noon. 'Getting abstract from safety deposit box.'

I sent a text back, 'Great, keep me posted.'

I got another text at 12:20, 'At the bank.'

I didn't reply.

Another text came thru at 12:25, 'Got abstract.'

I foolishly replied, 'Meet for dinner?'

She text me back at 12:27, 'Sure where?'

I text back, 'Shamrock's 6:00.'

12:31 Casey text back, 'Lol. No! Where else.'

I called her.

"Hi, Dev."

"Let me just state for the record that I'm a guy so I absolutely hate text messages. You pick the place."

"You hate texting because you're like all guys and you find it impossible to do two things at once."

"I'm looking out the window and talking to you on the phone, that's two things," I said.

"I'm not sure I could last an entire dinner with you if you think that's doing two things. How about La Grolla instead of Shamrock's."

"Works for me, is six okay?"

"It's perfect, see you then," she said.

Chapter Eighteen

La Grolla is a trendy Italian restaurant with nice wine, Italian beers and great food. It's also one of the 'in places' to be, so I called and made a reservation. I was seated near the window sipping my second beer when I checked my watch. Casey was only twenty-five minutes late. She must have learned her arrival time skills from Heidi.

I watched as she pulled up ten minutes later and attempted to parallel park. There was a good space and a half on the street. She backed in three separate times and hit the curb. I guess that was bound to happen each and every time if you don't readjust your wheels. After the third time she drove off down the street. The car that was waiting behind her pulled ahead and backed into the same spot. Then the guy got out and opened the door for a woman, probably his wife.

I took a couple sips from my beer, thought about ordering another, but decided to wait until Casey came in. The couple that had parked their car a moment ago was shown to a table across the room by the hostess. A moment later, a waiter was there with a basket of bread and menus, he appeared to take their drink order. He returned a few minutes later with a bottle of wine, opened it with a flourish and poured a little into the woman's glass. She tasted the wine, smiled, nodded, the waiter filled their glasses then left. They toasted one another and started talking.

Casey showed up a few minutes after that. "God, the parking is horrendous down here."

"Were there any spots out front?"

She shook her head. "My car wouldn't fit."

I decided to let it go and attend to the more pleasant aspects of the evening.

"Another beer, sir," our waiter asked.

I nodded.

"Madam?"

"I think a glass of wine."

"I'll spring for a bottle if you're interested."

"No, I'll just stick with the glass," she said then ordered a wine I couldn't pronounce.

"So you got it, your abstract?"

She nodded and pulled a document out of her purse. "Don't spill anything on this, Dev, it's the only copy and it's got stuff in there from before Minnesota was even a state, all the way back to the 1840's."

She had the thing wrapped in a Ziploc bag and passed it across the table to me like she was handing over a newborn infant. It was a dog-eared document with a faded green cover. I opened the first page and it led off with a legal property description from 1849. Minnesota didn't become a state until almost ten years later in 1858. Casey's home was built in 1885 by a guy named J. W. Stevens. His family apparently had it until 1916. I flipped through a number of pages, largely legal beagle stuff then I looked up at Casey.

"The last entry here is for 1983, Norman Speer. You didn't buy your house from the Speer family, did you?"

"I told you, I can't remember who we bought it from. I never met them, they weren't at the closing. It was just that sleazy lawyer guy."

"Jackie Van Dorn."

"Creepy Van Dorn, if you ask me."

"No argument from me, but he's not going to give us the seller's name, client privilege and all that stuff. Damn it, I thought the info would be on the property abstract."

Casey sort of rolled her eyes and said, "What? You've got to be kidding, Dev, they haven't been doing that since like forever. You're thinking back to the days when a bunch of little men with green visors and garters around their sleeves sat at high desks and wrote this stuff out under candlelight. Hello, time to update. God and you don't text either, surprise, surprise. It's all computerized now, time to move into the new century."

"Why even have this thing?" I said pointing to the abstract. "That's just great," I said, suggesting anything but, then took a healthy swallow of beer.

"Well, historical record just for a start, Dev. I thought that's why you wanted it, to get a little history of our house." Her eyes suddenly watered and she sounded on the verge of an emotional moment.

"It will be interesting to page through, Casey. I was just hoping to learn who you purchased the home from, that's all. I must not have made myself clear."

"Oh, you probably did, it's just that I've been such a wreck ever since…" and then her voice trailed off. Her face flushed and she bit her lower lip to keep in control.

I reached across the table and squeezed her hand. "I want to read this and Louie wanted to, too. You're right, it is interesting, it's just that there's no romance on the computer, at least for guys like me."

"Well, except for all the porn you probably watch," she laughed then took a sip of wine and seemed to get back under control.

"There is that," I said.

Chapter Nineteen

My back was to the office door when Louie came in. I had the binoculars up and was watching one of the women across the street making what looked to be a mug of tea. She had a short, silky sort of blue robe wrapped loosely around her and I could only hope the steam from the kettle would be so hot that she'd take the thing off. No such luck.

"That abstract from Casey is on your desk, there."

"Cool," Louie said then put his briefcase down, poured himself a mug of coffee and settled into his desk chair. He pulled the abstract out of the Ziploc bag.

"She's already yelled at me about spilling anything on it, so don't. Besides, it's not going to tell you a damn thing, anyway."

"I just love these things, they're such a slice of history, Dev. The day to day lives it reflects, the people that first settled here. Just think, no running water, no electricity, no phones."

"Yeah, sounds great, not." The woman across the way grabbed her mug and strutted sexily out of the kitchen. She began to remove her robe just as she walked into another room and vanished from sight.

I turned to face Louie. "I thought that thing would tell us who Casey and Dermot bought their house from, the thing is worthless on that count."

Louie stared at me for a long moment then said, "They haven't been listing that on abstracts for the last quarter of a century. Where have you been?"

"I've been busy."

"Starring out the window is what you've been doing. Staring as life just continues to pass you by, Dev. Come on, get with the program, hell, get with *any* program," he said then chuckled.

"How did we get from Casey's abstract to me being a bum? Don't answer that, and don't spill anything, damn it, she'll kill me."

Louie flipped the faded green cover back then nodded for a moment as he read. "Fantastic," he said to himself then looked up at me again. "That information, previous owners, taxes, valuation is a matter of public record."

"Yeah, I know that."

"Well, since you know that, then you probably also know you can go down to the Recorder's office and look it up, all you need is her property address."

It was so basic it hadn't occurred to me.

"I can see the light slowly coming on in that dim mind of yours, Dev."

"You know where they're located?"

"Hang on a sec, I know where they are, but let me get you the address." He hit a couple of keys on his computer waited a moment. "Here we go, PRR, 90 Plato Boulevard West, just go over the Wabasha Bridge and take a right."

"I'll be back," I said and headed out the door.

The Ramsey County Property Records and Revenue office is a fairly modern looking four-story, white stucco structure with lots of large windows and rounded corners on the entire exterior of the building.

The only county buildings I visited on any sort of a regular basis was either the courthouse or the jail. Just by the nature of the beast, the experience was likely to be on the unpleasant side. This was altogether different.

"Hi, how can I help you?" a pleasant looking woman, maybe in her fifties asked. Her name tag read 'Mary Jane.' We were standing at a long counter of laminated wood. She was on the business side of the counter and I was on the groveling side. The room was bright with floor to ceiling windows, off-white walls and fluorescent lights. Amazingly none of the lights were flickering. Framed and matted prints of various city scenes hung on the walls.

"I'd like to look up property records for a home in Saint Paul," I said.

"I'll just need an address and I can bring that tape out to you, everything is on micro fiche," she added sensing my bewilderment.

I gave her Casey's address and she directed me to a table divided into a number of individual cubicles. She brought out a roll of micro fiche to me just a few minutes later. "You need anything else just let me know. When you're finished here just bring the tape back up to the front desk. If you need copies made of any records we can do that for a modest fee."

"Thank you, I don't think copies will be necessary."

"The records are filed alphabetically by street name and then numerically based on address. So you'll be going to 'H' for Holly Avenue then numeric order after that, okay?"

"We'll see if I screw it up."

"I'm here if you do," she said.

"Thanks, Mary Jane."

"You're very welcome, Mr. Haskell."

"Please, call me, Dev."

"Okay, Dev," she smiled. "Let me know if you need anything else."

I nodded then watched her walk away wondering was that last line a come on? At the Records office? I didn't think so. Was it?

I landed on Casey's records in just a few minutes then slowly ran down the dates from the late eighteen hundreds through the last century. I paused at November, 1983 when Norman Speer purchased the property from a Richard Mallnory. Norman Speer sold to a guy named Lowell Bulski in 2006. Bulski sold to Dermot and Casey Gallagher in March of 2013. That was where Jackie Van Dorn got involved. It all pretty much dovetailed with what Casey's neighbor across the street and Casey herself had told me. Now I just had to find this Lowell Bulski and see if he had any sort of connection to Bulldog.

I removed the tape from the viewer and walked back to the front counter.

"That was fast," Mary Jane said looking up at me.

"That's because you gave me such good directions to begin with. Do you have records on individuals?"

"Individuals?"

"Yeah, if I got a guy's name would you have a record of where he lived, employment, you know, that sort of thing?"

"I do know and no we don't have records of that sort. You might want to try a phone book or you could go on line and possibly look that up in a reverse directory. If you have an address you might be able to learn who lived there. Word of advice, don't pay for any of that information. If they want to charge you just move on to another site. You might start online with 'White Pages'. They're a pretty intuitive site."

"White pages, I'll remember that. Thanks, Mary Jane, you've been a big help."

"Always my pleasure, stop in anytime," she smiled.

There it was again, was she or wasn't she?

Chapter Twenty

I phoned Louie as I pulled out of the parking lot.

"Yeah, Dev, what is it?"

"Just wanted to say thanks, I'm leaving your friends at PRR now."

"You get what you needed?"

"Yes and no. The good news is I got a name, the bad news is it doesn't mean a damn thing to me."

"Who is it?"

"Some guy named Lowell Bulski, ring any bells?"

"No, not off the top of my head. You got a second, I'm on my computer I could look him up."

"Yeah, please do." I was headed back across the Wabasha Bridge. I stopped for a red light at the far end of the bridge while Louie was clicking keys on his computer.

"Okay, here we go," he said just as the light turned green. "There's a guy with that same last name listed with the Liquor Board of Control out of Washington, the state not D.C. A Bulski contracting out of Milwaukee, a Florence Bulski, poet, but nothing with the first name Lowell. That's the guy's name, the guy your pals bought their house from?"

"Yeah, he's the guy Jackie Van Dorn covered for in the closing. I got an idea."

"If you're thinking of going to Van Dorn's office, don't. That's not a good idea."

"Relax, I have no intention of going to his office, I promise. I better ring off, I'm driving and I'm heading into some heavy construction."

"Later," Louie said and hung up.

The parking lot at Nasty's was more full than when I was here the other day. I found a place about as far away from the door as you could get. The same heavy-set woman was stuffed into the little glass booth just past the door. She had a cigarette almost burned down to the filter smoldering next to her. Her left shoulder and arm were flattened up against the bulletproof glass.

"Five bucks," she said not looking up from her book, it looked to be a different romance than the other day.

I slipped a ten into the little well in the counter. She gave half a sigh suggesting she really couldn't be bothered then after some effort she slid a five back out to me.

"Thank you very much," I said sweetly.

That got her going on a phlegmy coughing jag and I pushed the pair of brass boobs on the doors and fled inside. The place was more or less packed with guys in suits and loosened starched collars. I couldn't spot an open table. Occasionally, a whistle or two came from the crowd. The two women dancing on stage looked fairly happy with clumps of dollar bills stuffed in their garters, and the half dozen girls out on the floor working the crowd all had smiles on their faces.

I headed toward the bar.

The same crabby bartender from the other day looked over at me while pouring a tray of tap beers, at least this time she was actually doing something. "Yeah," she grunted.

"I'm looking for Freddy."

"That fat guy, the bouncer?"

"That's him."

"I think he woke up from his nap and left about half an hour ago. You might check the parking lot, he could be back asleep out there in his car."

Wow, she actually had a sense of humor. Then again, given it was Freddy we were talking about maybe she was just stating a fact. More whistles and yells from the crowd as the two girls dancing picked up cash from the guys seated along the edge of the stage.

The lights suddenly dimmed and a deep smoker's voice growled over the speakers. "And now the moment you've all been waiting for, Nasty's presents the nastiest star attraction you've ever seen, how about a warm welcome for Cougar. Take your hands out of your pants and give the clap to Cougar. Cougar. Cougar."

Apparently they liked it because the crowd went wild. Cheering, clapping, more loud sharp whistles. A good portion of the place was on their feet, a couple of guys stood on chairs to watch as Cougar strutted on stage then placed her hands on her hips and pretended to pull out guns, she shot into the crowd with both hands, pointing her index fingers and moving her thumbs like the hammer on a pistol. The crowd went crazy and there was a palpable surge toward the stage. Three well-muscled, thug-type bouncers sort of kept people back.

The thumping music started and Cougar danced across the stage, after about thirty seconds she took the scarf from around her neck, used it like a towel to rub her backside then tossed it into the crowd. There was a pushing match to get the damn thing. I had no doubt that just ninety minutes earlier most of these idiots were probably at their desk somewhere in a bank turning down first-time home buyers or charging exorbitant ATM fees.

"Grrr-rrrr, it's Cougar," the voice growled over the sound system and Cougar lowered her shoulder straps and shook her enhanced features from side to side.

That brought on more whistles and cat calls. I frankly didn't get it, but then again I knew her. Of course back when I knew her, she was going by a different name, Swindle Lawless. An out of work porn star who threatened to sue Heidi and me for rape or lack of payment. Neither charge was correct, but no good deed goes unpunished so based on the legal advice from Louie, I paid Swindle four or five hundred bucks just so she'd drop the charges.

The last I heard she was striping and then at the end of the day wanted all the girls to hold hands in a prayer service where she promised to save their souls. Not what most of them needed to hear at two-thirty in the morning. They either wanted to just get home or get with the paying customer out in the parking lot. I guessed timing had never really been Swindle's forte.

I tuned out the wolf whistles, the cat calls, the cheers and thought back to what Casey's across the street neighbor had said. *'There was one woman, strange sort of thing. Unbalanced might be the best word I can think of. Dressed like she was the worst sort of street person, but I heard from one of the neighbors she was some kind of missionary.'* It suddenly dawned on me, strange, unbalanced and some kind of missionary, it had to be Swindle. She was one of the renters that had turned Casey's home into the worst house on the block. No surprise. It seemed an odds-on possibility that Swindle could tell me something about the former owner, Lowell Bulski.

Chapter Twenty-One

It was getting late and I'd nursed three ten-dollar lite beers for the better part of five hours. I didn't know what I was more ashamed of, nursing the beer or the fact that they were lite. The crowd had finally thinned, the last of the bankers were in the process of dragging themselves home where they'd groan to their wives about working late hours and then fall asleep in front of the late night news.

Swindle aka Cougar had been working the crowd, giving lap dances and downing shots. I caught her eye while she was grinding away on some suit and scanning the crowd over his shoulder. She gave me an aggressive nod, pointed to me and mouthed the words, "You're next." Gee, I could hardly wait. She was staggering toward me a few minutes later.

"Hey, sugar, I'm all warmed up for you. What do say? You get comfy on that bar stool and for forty bucks I'll give you the time of your life," she said then struck a pose and half growled.

"Hey, Swindle, how's it going?"

She seemed to sag for half a moment then brightened. "Back for more are we. I knew it, couldn't get enough, could you? Tell me your name again, baby, you've got me so excited I can't even think straight."

"Yeah, I'm sure it's got nothing to do with the half dozen shots you did out there. I thought you went straight and were doing the Lord's work?"

"That wasn't any fun, forget that shit. So, you got forty bucks? Otherwise you're wasting my time. What'd you say your name was?"

"Haskell, Dev Haskell, we...."

"Sure I remember, sort of. Didn't we have a three-way, after the victory party for Gino D'Angelo? God, the victory that never, ever happened."

"It wasn't exactly a three-way, see..."

"Three, four what the hell difference does it make? They all run together." She slapped me on the chest then said, "Hey, just for old times sake, I'll give you a deal, let's call it even at forty bucks for the time of your life. What'd you say, Den?"

"It's Dev."

"Okay, whatever."

"How 'bout a shot, Swindle?"

"Sure is there a better way to get in the mood?" she said then nodded at the crabby bartender who was standing behind me at the bar. She pulled an already poured shot off a tray next to the cash register and handed it to Swindle.

Swindle downed the thing in a nano-second, shuddered then put the empty shot glass on the bar.

The bartender took a ten off my stack of cash.

"Woo-hoo-hoo, you got me cooking now, Danny boy."

"It's Dev, Swindle, I just wanted to talk to you for a minute if I could."

She grinned and shook her chest from side to side. "Call it anything you like, baby," she half slurred then signaled Crabby for another shot.

"Did you used to live on Holly Avenue?" I asked.

She tossed the shot back then looked like she was trying to think for a minute, maybe reach back through her alcohol induced haze. "I don't know any guy named Holly," she said then signaled for another shot and downed the thing before I even realized it had been passed to her.

"Oh, God that is bitching. Come on, Dave, you gotta let me do it, my treat, forty bucks, what do say, baby?" She sort of staggered back a step or two then slid her hand down her hip and inside her thong. "I'm gonna shoot you baby," she said then attempted to pull her hand out. A ring caught on her thong and she half struggled with her hand then suddenly staggered to the side. I caught her by the shoulder and straightened her up so she didn't fall.

"Swindle, do you know a guy named Lowell Bulski?" I asked, just as a pair of very large hands grabbed me and put a vice grip on my upper arm.

"No touching the main attraction, douche bag."

I turned to stare into the muscled chest of a very large man. I looked up into his face and recognized him as one of the thugs that had held the crowd of bankers back a few hours earlier. Tribal tattoos were wrapped around his very large biceps and he increased the pressure on his grip.

"She was starting to fall and I just stopped her from going over. Tubby and Bulldog asked me to come in and keep an eye on her tonight."

That seemed to get him thinking and he let go of my arm. "We ain't heard nothing about that," he said, but he didn't sound all that sure.

"Go check it out, maybe one of the others knows. Or give Tubby a call. I think Bulldog talked to Fat Freddy this afternoon. I was with him when he made the call, for Christ's sake."

"I'll check it out, ah sorry 'bout that." He nodded and slowly backed away.

"Not a problem, I'll put in a good word," I said then turned back to Swindle, just as she was handing another empty shot glass back to Crabby.

"Swindle, you were telling me about Lowell Bulski."

"He's gonna be with us, too? God, he never pays and I'm not giving both of ya's freebies," she said.

"You know him?" I said then saw the bouncer from a moment earlier talking to the other two bouncers, they were shaking their heads and then suddenly all three looked back over in my direction.

"Hunh?"

"I said do you know him? Lowell Bulski?"

"You kiddin'? Bulldog? Everyone knows that prick. He likes it a little rough, but I don't care he can just..."

The three of them started to move from the edge of the stage and head my way. A table of a half dozen guys in suit coats suddenly started to get up and the three thugs had to wait a half moment. That was all the time I needed to start my traveling music.

I went to grab my money off the bar, there were only three dollar bills sitting there. "Hey," I said to Crabby. "I had about fifty or sixty bucks sitting on the bar a moment ago."

"It was sixty, actually. Swindle's shots are ten bucks each, you owe me another ten," she said.

The table of bankers had cleared and the bouncers were on the move again. I pulled a folded ten from a wad in Swindle's garter and tossed it on the bar.

Swindle looked like she might be trying to think of a protest, but her eyes were already glazed over at half mast and she was too far gone. She put her hands on her hips and attempted to strike a pose which caused her to stagger a couple of steps into another table where she knocked over a beer. I didn't wait to see what happened after that.

I was pulling out of Nasty's parking lot and glanced in the rearview mirror just as one of those bouncers stepped out the front door and looked around. He did not appear to be happy.

Chapter Twenty-Two

It was seven-thirty in the morning and I was sitting in Aaron LaZelle's office, my Lieutenant pal in homicide. I'd brought a couple of caramel rolls from Nina's just to sweeten the meeting. We were eating them with our fingers, both of us trying to cover the aftertaste from the vending machine coffee.

"So, you were just on your way home from another night of debauchery and decided to stop by?"

I looked around Aaron's cramped office. The thing was bounded on three sides by windows. One side looked out over the dumpsters behind the building and the other two sides looked into a room full of gray-blue cubicles. All the windows had a four-dollar set of plastic blinds hanging halfway down.

"What the hell do you do if you ever want to be private in here?"

"It's really complicated, I just pull the blinds. Those babies are down, believe me everyone stays clear."

I nodded, it seemed to make sense. I'd been on the receiving end of more than one interrogation by Aaron.

"So, is there a purpose to our chance early morning meeting in my office?" he said, and brushed the crumbs off his desk and into his hand, then he tossed them into the wastebasket.

"I've been doing some checking around on Dermot Gallagher's…"

"Damn it, Dev I told you in no uncertain terms not to get involved. Exactly what part of 'stay the hell away' don't you understand? I don't want you anywhere near…"

"Whoa, will you just calm down. I didn't do anything other than look at some records."

"Records?" he asked and the flushed face from a moment before began to return back to normal.

"Yeah, I'm sleeping there, at Casey's and Dermot's."

"Please tell me you two aren't shacking up."

"You kidding? Give the woman some credit. She's got a little higher standards than sleeping with someone like me. No, she was just uncomfortable being there and then she was worried about someone casing the place and breaking in so I told her I'd stay there."

"You actually did something nice?"

"Yeah, I know, even I was kind of surprised."

"And you were there reviewing records?"

"Yeah, but not there, I went down to PRR to check out their records."

"And?"

"The name Lowell Bulski ring any bells?"

"The Bulldog? You ran into that ass at PRR?"

"What? No, of course not, but I did find out that he was the guy that sold the house to Casey and Dermot. Let me rephrase that, he was the owner of record, he wasn't at the closing. He was represented at the closing by an attorney, Jackie Van Dorn."

"God, *that* sleaze bag."

"That seems to be the general consensus. I just thought if you guys weren't aware of that it certainly seems to be an interesting little bit of trivia. Maybe a direction you might consider looking into if you haven't already."

Aaron nodded. "They had been in that place for a couple of years, right?"

"Almost two-and-a-half. It was pretty torn up when Dermot was murdered, some sort of a major project going on in just about every room and they were the worker-bees, if that translates."

Aaron nodded.

"It's even crazier now, she's got to sell the place, can't make the payments on her own and well, frankly, I think she's just damn uncomfortable there. She's staying at one of her brothers' for the time being. Contractors are in there from seven-thirty in the morning to five at night, banging, sawing, welding, God, I've been at the office before nine just about every morning."

"Gee, starting at nine, you early bird. I'm sure you're loving that."

"Not really. Anyway, I was sort of wondering if you'd have anything on your pal Bulldog."

"Have anything?" Aaron asked then started clicking keys on his computer.

"Yeah, like where he might have been when the sale of that house was going down. Why he wasn't there."

Aaron sort of gave a disgusted smirk then nodded and clicked a few more keys. "Here we go, Bulski, yeah, I'm guessing they maybe bought that place in late 2012 or early 2013?"

"Yeah, sounds about right."

"Bulldog was on a sabbatical."

A sabbatical?"

"Yeah, Lino Lakes, he was doing eighteen months for a possession with intent to distribute charge."

"Eighteen months seems like kind of a light sentence for him."

"You can thank the winning combination of our enlightened judiciary and the lawyerly skills of Councilor Van Dorn."

"So that's why he wasn't around?"

"Might also be why he sold."

"How's that?"

"He's locked up for a period of time, even so he's got some obligations I would guess, on and no doubt, off the books. It may be why Van Dorn was involved although I'd be willing to guess the association with Tubby Gustafson probably had more to do with it. You remember a thug named George Marcela?"

"Yeah, wasn't he called Georgie Boy?"

"That was his nice side, his other name was 'Chopper,' for obvious reasons."

I gave Aaron a look.

"Lets just say he had a fetish for hands, you crossed him and he'd cut off your hand."

"Charming."

Aaron nodded. "Maybe three months before Bulldog gets sentenced Marcela disappears. There've been rumors we pick up from time to time that he skipped town and now he's in Vegas, LA, maybe Miami someplace like that, but we never hear anything concrete. When he supposedly skipped town he apparently took a lot of cash with him, close to half a million dollars."

"Let me guess, the money belonged to Tubby Gustafson."

"Right, or that's at least who we think it belonged to."

"I got two problems with that, the first is that's a nice bit of change to you and me, but its chump change for these guys. Five hundred grand? And you're on the run? Where is he gonna go and be safe, nowhere. I don't think a guy like Marcela would do that for ten times the amount, it would be stupid. And then, what does this have to do with Bulldog?"

"Supposedly Marcela was the supplier, it's how Bulldog actually gets involved with Tubby's inner circle business. Marcela disappears, Bulldog serves eighteen months because he won't cop a plea and finger Tubby's organization, by the way he does the time standing on his head. So, he gets out and immediately steps into Marcela's old job as enforcer for Tubby Gustafson."

"Nice work if you can get it," I said.

"Not really. Just for the record, suppose Bulldog took out Marcela and grabbed Tubby's five hundred grand. I'm guessing that would put him on some pretty thin ice, probably get him killed."

"One can only hope they'd give him a long, painful death," I said.

"Nothing has ever been proven, in fact, a lot of it is just supposition on our part. I mean a flip side of it could be Tubby asked Bulldog to take out Marcela with the promise of making him enforcer and sweetening the pot with the five hundred grand."

"I've never really thought of Tubby as being that generous," I said.

"Well, there is that. Look, I had better get to work, was there anything else?" Aaron asked.

"No, I'd just encourage you guys to take a long, hard look at Bulldog on this thing and just pursue it until you get whoever the bastard was that killed Dermot."

"That's exactly what we've been doing, Dev."

Chapter Twenty-Three

"So that's what they're going to do, check out Bulldog's perfect alibi?" Louie had to shout so I could hear him.

We were sitting in a far back booth at The Spot. There was a large crowd of women drinking glasses of white wine or pink and blue drinks and they were all clustered around the bar. Some sort of pre-party to a twenty-year high school reunion. They all looked like they were glad to flee the kids and leave the little darlings with their husbands for the night. The noise level was about ten decibels above permanent deafness.

"There has to be a tie-in somewhere, it's just too coincidental, Bulldog owning the place they end up buying and then Dermot's killed," I said.

"But what would be in it for him?"

"What?"

"What's in it for him, for Bulldog?"

"I don't know," I shrugged.

"You think he wanted the house back?"

"I think if he wanted it back he could have made them an offer and they would have at least entertained the idea. Just looking around over there, I'd say they were overwhelmed with major projects throughout the entire house. Probably no time to finish them and even less money."

"It's still awfully strange," Louie said.

"It's one of those coincidences that I can't believe is just a coincidence."

"What?" Louie said.

I just shouted, "Yes" and nodded at the same time.

A few minutes later the crowd began to disperse, heading out the front and side doors on to the next venue wherever that was. It was suddenly blissfully quiet.

"Let's grab a stool," Louie said sliding out of the booth. "You better give us another round," Louie said to Jimmy a moment later.

He just looked at us and smiled.

"Jimmy, Jimmy," Louie said and snapped his fingers to get Jimmy's attention.

Jimmy grinned then pulled a pair of yellow foam ear plugs out of ears. "Thank God," he said, "I'd be permanently damaged if it wasn't for these things."

"Give us a round," Louie said. We sat and sipped and contemplated some of the finer things in life, like the next round.

The flat screens were on in the two corners above the bar, tuned to the baseball game. The sound had been muted when the loud crowd had been in earlier and Jimmy had never turned it back up. That was okay, the Twins were getting spanked by Chicago. It was bad enough giving the game the occasional glance and catching the score. I didn't need to hear how bad things were going, too. Mercifully the disaster came to a close and five minutes of commercials started up. The first was for the ten o'clock news.

The screen was filled with the photo of a heavyset guy with a blond Mohawk. He was leaning against a picnic table and appeared to be shouting and waving what looked like a large turkey drumstick. The caption across the bottom of the screen read 'Assault Victim.' The photo looked an awful lot like Fat Freddy.

"Jimmy, turn up the sound will ya, I think I know that guy," I said.

"Let me just find where I left that damn remote, Dev," he said walking down the length of the bar looking from left to right. He eventually found it next to the pull-tab box and turned up the sound just as the news broadcast began.

"Police tonight are looking for four men involved in the vicious daylight assault that occurred about three-thirty this afternoon in the parking lot of Nasty's. Apparently the victim, thirty-one year old Fredrick Zimmerman was assaulted while on the way to his car. Zimmerman, an employee of Nasty's is listed in stable condition tonight at Regions Hospital. Police are asking anyone with information to please contact them."

"In other news the Twins suffered yet another defeat…"

"Is that…?"

"…Fat Freddy," I answered. "I was just with him a couple of days ago. Jesus Christ."

"Someone beat him up in the middle of the afternoon in Nasty's parking lot?" Louie said.

"Yeah, and I'm willing to bet I know exactly who had a hand in it if he didn't attack him outright."

"Who?"

"Bulldog."

"Hey, look, Dev. I know you were kind of warming to Fat Freddy and you are no fan of Bulldog's. By the way, neither am I, but it might be a little farfetched to pin this on him."

"Not a fan? No, I'll lay you odds on it, he's responsible. I just know it."

"How can you be so sure?"

"Because it's my fault."

"What are you talking about?"

"I was at Nasty's the other night. I went in there to talk to Fat Freddy, to see if he could tell me who Lowell Bulski is."

"That name you got off the property records at PRR? I checked online and couldn't find anything. Remember?"

"Yeah, but just 'cause it's not online doesn't mean there aren't other sources."

"Now Fat Freddy is a source?"

"I had a hunch, Bulski, Bulldog, get it?"

"No."

"Bulski, the last name, it's why that bastard Bulldog is called Bulldog, well, that and the fact the guy is such an asshole."

"And Freddy told you this?"

"No, as a matter of fact, I never even talked to Freddy, never saw him, he'd already left. The place was jammed with all sorts of upstanding citizens and 'swells' getting their fill. Then this chick came on the stage, they hyped her as the nastiest woman Nasty's has ever had or something like that. She was clearly the reason all the suits were there. Anyway, she does a couple of half-ass numbers then is out fleecing the crowd for lap dances. Can you believe she get's forty bucks?"

"So who was she?"

"I'm getting to that. I can't get near her for a couple of hours. They got these big, thuggy bouncers literally guarding her ass. She's out there doing lap dances and shit, she's on some guy and at the same time signaling me that I'm next. You know who it was?"

"I got no idea."

"The name Swindle Lawless ring any bells?"

"You are kidding me, Swindle Lawless? That porn star slut who was with Tommy and Gino D'Angelo until they got sent to prison? Do you mean to tell me she hasn't died from some sort of overdose or been run over by a group of enraged wives? God, the female version of Keith Richards and she's still out there proving everyone wrong. I don't believe it."

"Believe it. She tossed down seven or eight shots while I tried to talk to her. Ten bucks a crack."

"That's what she charges?"

"No, that's what the shots cost."

"God. So what does any of this have to do with your husky friend Freddy being put in the hospital?"

"Oh yeah, so I'm trying to talk with her, asking if she knows who Lowell Bulski is? I'm thinking she may have lived at Casey's when it was cut into sleazy apartments. One of the neighbors I talked to described a woman who lived there as strange and unbalanced."

"That could be just about any woman who would go out with you."

"I'm asking old Swindle if she knows Lowell and she's kind of drunk and sort of staggers. I had to grab her by the shoulders so she wouldn't fall. Next thing I know some bouncer wants to throw me out. So, I told him Tubby and Bulldog sent me over to watch Swindle and they had told Fat Freddy to pass on the info to the rest of the bouncers. Anyway, that bouncer checks with his pals, they start to come after me and that's when I just got the hell out of there. Long way around the barn, but I think that's why Freddy was attacked and I'd be willing to bet Bulldog had something major to do with it."

"So now what?"

"I think I'll finish this beer and head back to Casey's place. Maybe go see Freddy in the hospital tomorrow morning."

"You think that's wise?"

"I doubt Tubby or Bulldog will be there at his bedside. I just might cheer him up, you never know."

Chapter Twenty-Four

Regions Hospital is located on the northern edge of downtown Saint Paul just across from the Minnesota State Capitol complex. The facility covers two blocks and rises up nine stories. I stopped at the information desk in the front lobby to get directions up to Fat Freddy's room.

"Are you with the newspaper?" the woman asked. Her volunteer nametag said 'Eleanor' and she flashed me the briefest of smiles that disappeared almost before it began.

"No, just a friend," I replied.

"Mmm-mmm," she murmured suggesting I was a disappointment and held no further interest then she gazed past me into the lobby indicating I was dismissed.

I made my way down the hall, onto the elevator and up to the third floor. Freddy's room was two right turns, a left turn, then down a hallway to another right turn then straight ahead. I'd need a compass just to find my way back. I would have dropped breadcrumbs except that the maintenance staff was waxing the hall floor so my effort would have been for naught.

I half expected a police officer or some sort of security to be sitting in front of his room. There wasn't any. No one questioned me as I entered the room. The bed was raised so Freddy was able to sit. He was propped up by three or four additional pillows and just staring out the window at his personal view of the interstate. His powder blue hospital gown seemed to contrast with his bruised arms and his swollen black and blue face.

A shiny metal sort of splint was positioned over his nose then covered with gauze and layers of white adhesive tape. The right ear where I'd pulled the gauge from his ear lobe a couple weeks back had been reinjured and looked like a giant tooth hanging on the side of his head. The massive ear lobe was split and dangled in an inverted 'V' like the roots of an extracted tooth. His eyes seemed to flutter like he was fighting sleep and losing the battle.

There were two IV bags dripping into a tube attached to his left hand. I guessed one was probably some sort of pain medication and the other maybe just fluid to help keep him hydrated.

"How's it going, Freddy?"

"Kinda horseshit right now," he mumbled. When he spoke he made an effort not to move his swollen lips.

"What the hell happened?"

"I got no idea. Bulldog said he had information I was trying to move in on one of their stars."

"One of their stars?"

"That old witch Cougar. I guess she told him or something. I don't know what the hell she's talking 'bout. She ain't said more than two words to me in all the time I been there."

Swindle, it figured.

"The night crew said some guy told them he cleared talking to Cougar with me. I don't know nothing about any of that. I kept telling them I didn't talk to anyone and that's when they started kicking the shit out of me. Bastards didn't stop for a hell of a long time. Then Bulldog walks up, tells me I'm fired and kicks me some more. Shit, the son-of-a-bitch coulda just sent a text message," he said then looked like he might smile, but thought better of it.

"I saw it on the news, last night. Hell of a way to get free press," I joked.

"You're telling me."

"Well look, I just wanted to see if you were alive, it looked pretty bad watching TV."

"Think I might be a star?" He sounded halfway hopeful.

"Maybe not just yet, Freddy."

"Shit," he said and then his eyes started to flutter until they gradually closed. I checked the pulse monitor just to make sure he was still alive then pulled a business card out of my wallet and placed it on the bed table in front of him. I only made one wrong turn on my way back to the elevators then drove to the office.

"Sleeping in," Louie asked when I came through the door, then he went back to the files spread across the picnic table in front of him.

"Actually, I was down at Regions, visiting Fat Freddy."

Louie sat back in his chair and tossed his pen on the pad in front of him. "How bad is it?"

"Bad enough, but he'll live. I don't think anything was broken." I said then settled into my chair, picked up the binoculars and scanned the building across the street.

"Did you even ask if anything was broken?"

112

"He was on meds, pain killers most likely, God the poor bastard fell asleep while he was talking to me."

"I'm not sure that's the fault of the meds."

"He was black and blue, swollen, had a splint on his nose and maybe some teeth knocked out, but he'll live."

"Jesus."

"Oh, and get this, they fired him."

"Who fired him?"

"Bulldog, it was him and that night crew of bouncers that assaulted Freddy."

"They physically assaulted another employee, in broad daylight, in the company parking lot?"

"Yeah, and then fired him."

"God, I'd like to sue that organization."

"I don't think that's exactly how they settle their 'issues,' Louie."

"Well, yeah, but Jesus."

I set the binoculars down and turned back to face Louie. "You know, there might be a silver lining here, an opportunity."

"How's that?"

"I'm not sure yet, I just have a feeling." I said then turned round and scanned the third floor again. I thought the refrigerator door might look like it was open when suddenly a girl stood up from behind the kitchen counter. She had a towel wrapped around her head and was wearing a smile. My luck was definitely changing.

Chapter Twenty-Five

My positive vibe was relatively short lived. I was in the den at Casey's sipping a cranberry juice because I'd run out of beer and the liquor stores were closed. I'd called Heidi to see if she wanted to come over and misbehave, but she was getting ready for a hot date. I was watching the Twins slowly being beaten to death, one long inning at a time. There had been a light rain falling, unfortunately not heavy enough to call the game. My phone rang. I could only hope it was Heidi calling to tell me her hot date had turned out to be gay.

"Haskell Investigations."

"Dev?" Casey's voice cried from the other end of the phone.

"Casey? What's wrong?"

"Someone ran into my car and they're towing it away. It's all smashed up and wrecked."

"Are you okay?"

"I think so, but my car, what am I going to do?"

"Where are you?"

"I'm at University and Western, in front of some big old empty building."

I knew exactly where she was, it was an old bakery building from the 1930's. There was a Green Line stop there, our attempt at light rail. Not the best corner for a woman to be on foot after dark unless she was working the street.

"I'm going to come and get you, I'm about ten minutes away."

"God, Dev, what else can go wrong? My life is just shit," she sobbed.

"You just hang on, Casey. I'm coming."

I dashed out the door, climbed in my car and took off. I probably made it in six minutes, only because the cops didn't nail me for speeding. I saw her standing on the corner looking very distraught. Her arms were folded across her chest and she was obviously crying. The car ahead of me slowed down like they were going to stop then sped up once they got a closer look at her. I pulled to the curb and got out.

She saw it was me, but remained where she was and started shaking her head from side to side. First her shoulders started shuddering and then her entire body followed suit. I hurried over to her.

"Dev," was all she said and then she just broke down and sobbed uncontrollably. All I could do was wrap my arms around her and hold her as she released a flood of emotion. After all she'd been through, all she'd lost, Dermot, their house, what she knew as her life, this was where she finally cracked, on the corner of University and Western, late at night with the light rail clanging its bell as it passed through the intersection and I was the guy holding her in the rain. Life ain't fair.

After a bit she regained control and pushed herself back. "Oh, God, I'm so sorry. Look at me, I'm just a mess. God, how can you stand me? How can anyone?"

"You're okay, Casey, that's the important thing. You're not hurt, are you?"

She shook her head. "No, I'm okay, well except that I'm royally fucked. God," she said then looked to be on the verge of breaking down again. I wrapped my arms around her and said, "You're what's important, you can always get another car." Some jerk driving past leaned on his horn and let it blare for another half-a-block.

"Come on let's get you in my car before all these guys driving by start hitting on you."

"You kidding? I look like shit," she said and sniffled.

"I think you're beautiful," I said.

"That just proves you're not in your right mind."

I held the door open for her and she slid into the passenger seat.

"Buckle up now, you've had enough excitement for one night."

"You think it would make any difference at this point?" she said then pulled the seat belt across her. I ignored her comment and waited until I heard the buckle click then closed her door and hurried over to the driver's side. I started the car then pushed the button to lock our doors.

"Where to, Madam?"

"Can you take me to Tommy's, Dev? Jesus, I must really look like shit. Sorry for that back there, I just sort of snapped."

"I think under the circumstances you may be entitled. Hey, if you open that glove compartment I think there's some Kleenex in there."

She opened the glove compartment and the box of Kleenex sort of slid halfway out. Two wrapped condoms lay next to it.

"Oh, back to dating high school girls are we?"

"Oh, sorry about that," I said.

116

She just shook her head and smiled.

I drove around the block and headed back in the general direction of Casey's house although I didn't think that would be a very good idea. "You want me to take you to Tommy's?"

"Yeah, I guess. I don't know what else I can do. I just can't think right now. That guy had to have seen me, and he just plowed into me, didn't even slow down. What a complete and utter…"

"Don't worry about any of that right now. We'll get it sorted out, let the police deal with it. Where does Tommy live?"

"Hunh? Oh yeah, I guess that would help, wouldn't it?" she said then gave me his address.

We pulled up in front of her brother's house fifteen minutes later. It was a nice looking Cape Cod-style two-story house with a brick front and a trimmed hedge running across the front. An attached two-stall garage was on the right hand side. There was a light post halfway up the curved front sidewalk with the light on and a plaque with the address numbers. Other than an outside light over the front door the rest of the house was dark.

"God, I hate when they go out and don't leave any lights on. They went to a concert or something tonight."

I nodded then got out and walked her to the door.

"I guess I can make it from here," she said reaching a tentative arm inside and flicking on the light. There were actually three light switches and she turned on all three. One went on just inside the front door, another lit up an area at the base of the staircase running up to the second floor and the third light was inside the front hall closet. Casey didn't look all that thrilled.

"How 'bout if I walk through the place just to make sure you're okay?"

"Oh, God, would you mind?"

"Not a problem, I'd be happy to, in fact, I insist."

"Do you have a gun?"

"I think I can manage," I said and stepped in past her. She followed behind me.

I turned on lights as we walked from the front entry, through the dining room and into the kitchen. At the back door I turned on the exterior lights and illuminated the well-kept backyard. "Let me check the basement, Casey. I'll be back up in a moment."

She nodded and looked relieved. The basement was a refinished den with a giant flat screen on the wall over a wood burning fireplace. What looked like high school graduation pictures of two girls were framed and sitting on the fireplace mantel. Off that room was a laundry area and workbench next to the furnace. I came back upstairs just as Casey was opening one of the kitchen cabinets. I noticed she'd turned on two additional lamps in the living room, the lights in a china cabinet in the dining room and the light in the small bathroom that was just off the kitchen.

"Could I talk you into a glass of wine?" she asked, there was just the hint of a plea in her voice.

"I'd like that, let me just walk through the upstairs and I'll be right down."

"God, I feel like such a dope making you do all this, Dev."

"Forget it, you've had a pretty busy night, you just take care of that wine and I'll be right back down."

I open and closed the doors on the second floor so it sounded like I was being thorough, but I wasn't going to go into the bedrooms looking in closets and under the beds. I came down the stairs and walked back to the kitchen. Casey had the foil around the neck of the wine bottle partially torn off and lying on the Formica

118

counter. She had the arms on the cork screw lifted up and was attempting to uncork the bottle, it wasn't working.

"God I hate these things. Why don't they just buy the damn bottles with the screw off caps? It's so much easier."

"Can I give you a hand?" I said and took the corkscrew from her, lowered the arms then turned the handle making the arms raise.

"Why wouldn't it work for me?"

"You just had the arms already up and it doesn't work that way." The cork rose three-quarters of the way out of the bottle then I pulled it out the rest of the way. It made a satisfied popping sound. "Should we let it breathe for a moment?"

"No," Casey said with some authority then grabbed the wine bottle from me. She filled her glass then mine, picked up the bottle along with her glass and marched into the living room.

I followed.

There were two small couches facing each other on either side of the living room, a glass topped coffee table was positioned between them. Casey set the wine bottle on the coffee table and curled up in the corner of a couch. I sat down opposite her. She took about three healthy gulps from her glass then closed her eyes and twisted her head from side to side.

"What a day, Jesus wept," she said then drank a little more wine although this time it was more of a demure sip.

"You feel like talking about the accident?"

"What's to tell? Some stupid idiot guy came around the corner and plowed into me."

"You think he was drunk or asleep, any idea?"

"Not the faintest. Who the hell knows? To tell you the truth I was sort of nervous, I thought some creep was following me, but he turned off into that restaurant parking lot just as I stopped for the red light. A half minute later some car comes around the corner and plows right into me. I think I panicked or something and tried to get out of the way. I must have because my car jumped forward and then he smashed into me. The idiot hit me at about my back tire, the air bag went off and knocked me down onto the seat. He pushed my car up over the curb and into a phone pole. Then he took off, he had to be drunk or high on something. I'm sure my car's totaled. Shit," she said then took another healthy swallow of wine and shook her head.

"What did the cops say?"

"What could they say? They got the tow truck there, told me my car was probably totaled and that based on the damage, I was really lucky. God, if they only knew," she said and drained her glass.

"You got any idea what the car looked like that hit you, or maybe the driver?"

Casey shook her head and reached for the bottle. "More wine?"

"No thanks, I still got this glass going."

She refilled her glass then set the bottle back on the coffee table. "The cops asked me the same thing. To tell you the truth, it all happened so fast I have no idea. I can't tell you if it was a man or a woman driving. I don't know if there was anyone else in the car. It was just a pair of headlights and then boom."

She raised her head for a moment like she was thinking then closed her eyes. "Oh, God, you'll just freak at this. I think it was a black car. God, do you believe it? What the hell is it with me and black cars?" she said then took a couple of healthy swallows.

"You mean like the car you thought was casing your house?" I laughed, but I was thinking it might not be that far fetched. Someone could have taken Fat Freddy's car, God knew he wasn't going to be using it for a while.

"Yeah sort of, I mean, look I honestly don't know, everything happened so damn fast. I just don't know what the hell I'm going to do for a car now."

"Well, you know you've got Dermot's car just sitting in the garage over at your place. It's pretty late tonight, but I could bring you over there tomorrow and you could get it."

"Do you think he'd mind?"

I wasn't sure how to respond to that and waited for her to catch herself, but she just looked at me with questioning eyes.

"I think he'd want you to, Casey. Dermot would have been the first one to tell you to use it."

She nodded and took another sip of wine.

I changed the subject. "How's the work going on the house? I gotta tell you they're in there bright and early everyday, bunch of guys working."

"It's coming along. I hope it's not too messy over there for you, Dev."

"I most likely wouldn't notice."

Casey nodded like that was probably an accepted fact. "You know, I'm going to hate to leave the place. I didn't think I would ever want to go back in there, but now I don't know. It was what we were doing, kind of our statement and I just don't know."

"Do you want to move back in?"

"No, I'm not ready for that, yet. Besides, like you said, the guys working and everything over there. No, I'm settled here for right now and I'm over there everyday, anyway. It's just, God, I wish I had the money, you know."

"Yeah, believe me I know how that works."

A pair of headlights drove up the driveway and a moment later we heard the garage door opening.

"Oh, here's Tommy and Carol home," Casey said, but she made no effort to get up. A door in the kitchen opened a minute later and we could hear them coming in from the garage.

"All the lights," a female voice said.

"We're in the living room," Casey called before anything else was said.

They walked into the living room and Tommy introduced me to his wife who I recognized from Dermot's funeral, but had never officially met. Casey gave them the quick version of the accident and Carol went out to the kitchen to grab two glasses and another bottle of wine. I declined any more wine and waited a requisite ten minutes before I made my good-byes. I told Casey I'd call her in the morning before I picked her up. Thanks were exchanged all around and I beat a hasty retreat back to Casey's house. Now it was my turn to feel nervous and I went through all the rooms, but this time I carried my .38.

Chapter Twenty-Six

"Oh sorry, didn't know anyone was in here," a guy in white pants and a white T-shirt said. He wore a baseball cap on his head with 'Abbott Paint' written across the crown. He was carrying a five-gallon bucket and a couple of trowels. I heard two other guys chuckle as he stepped back into the hallway. It was almost seven-thirty in the morning.

I put the coffee on, looked at myself in the mirror and decided whatever needed to be done could wait. I started to come alive after the third cup and phoned Aaron LaZelle in homicide. I had to leave a message. I showered, had another cup of coffee, and was driving to the office when my cell rang.

"Haskell Investigations."

"Were you planning to show up with caramel rolls again?" Aaron asked.

"No, one is all you get."

"Pity. Anyway, you called."

"Yeah, it may be nothing, but I know how we both feel about coincidences."

"Some woman you dated has turned up pregnant?"

"No, thank God. Casey Gallagher."

"Yes," Aaron drew out the word and I was willing to bet that he had just sat up straight in his office chair, maybe picked up a pen and slid a pad in front of him so he could take some notes.

"She was involved in a hit and run last night at the corner of University and Western."

"She okay?"

"Yeah, seems to be, other than the idiot totaled her car. I picked her up and brought her to her brother's where she's been staying, he lives over in the Como area. Anyway, here's the deal, bear with me. She thought she was being followed, she would have been heading north on Western. Then, as the light on University turns red and she stops, the car behind her turns into the parking lot behind a restaurant."

"It's a Vietnamese restaurant, right?"

"You got it. Less than a minute later, some car comes charging around the corner and broadsides her, slams her car into a phone pole and then takes off. That parking lot, it's L- shaped so someone could have turned in there, gone around the restaurant building, back onto University then blasted around the corner and hit her."

"Yeah, and it also could have been some idiot who was drinking or lost control or was underage who hit her. We'll check into it, but it could really just be unfortunate timing."

"There might be more."

"Such as?"

"Fat Freddy."

"What about him?" Aaron sounded cautious.

"He was assaulted coming out of Nasty's the other day by someone or a number of someone's, they put him in the hospital."

"Yeah, we're aware of that."

124

"I went to see him."

"You did what? Didn't we have a little chat about this sort of thing? You not screwing up an ongoing investigation, you not getting involved and making things even more difficult than they already are."

"There's a possibility it may have been his car that broadsided Casey last night."

"I believe he's still in Regions and pretty well banged up. He'll probably be there for at least another day or maybe two."

"Yeah, but his car isn't. It was parked at Nasty's, in their parking lot. I've a hunch if you got his license number and did a check you wouldn't find it parked there. It's a black Camaro, Z-18 or something. Casey made an offhanded comment that she thought it was a black car that hit her."

"Anything else?" I could tell by his tone he was writing and not very pleased.

"Not right now. I hear anything else you'll be the first person I call."

"I appreciate that, Dev, and thanks for passing on this information. Oh, and now lets get back to you not getting involved, please."

"You know me."

"Yeah, that's why I would appreciate you not screwing things up any further," he said and hung up.

Louie wasn't in the office when I got there. But, he had apparently been there earlier because the coffee pot was empty and still turned on. I smelled that electric burning smell the moment I walked in the door. I turned the pot off and checked the time, barely nine-thirty. I scanned the building across the street for the next half hour to no avail then called Casey and left a message.

Chapter Twenty-Seven

Fat Freddy told me it was Bulldog and the bouncers that beat him up. Aaron might have been playing coy, but I was willing to bet the police didn't have that bit of information. I thought it might be a good idea to bring Freddy some flowers, on my way I drove through Nasty's parking lot.

Even at this hour of the morning, there were patrons cars parked in the lot and the neon red 'open' sign was flashing next to the door. One could only hope the guys in there had been working third shift and stopped for just one on their way home. I drove through the lot twice, including taking a peek back by the dumpsters and the entrance to Jackie Van Dorn's office. The one thing I didn't see anywhere in the lot was Freddy's sinister looking black Camaro.

I checked at the hospital information desk just to make sure Freddy was still in the same room, he was. I picked up the cheapest flowers they had in the hospital gift shop, they were still overpriced. I eventually found my way to Freddy's room up on the third floor.

He was sitting up in bed working his way through three pancakes and watching the flat screen mounted up on the wall, it was tuned to Sesame Street.

He still looked pretty rough, but it was an improvement from the other day. The swelling had gone down, the bruises on his arms had lost their purple cast and were now a dull black. He still had the splint covering his nose, but I thought there might have been a little less gauze and tape. His eyes were still purple, but the swelling had gone down by half. His lips were bruised, but moving as he chewed. He still had that ugly ear.

"What the hell do you want?"

"Is that any way to treat someone who's bringing you flowers?"

"Those are for me?" he said sounding genuinely surprised.

"No, I saw them in the shop and just couldn't live without them. Yeah, they're for you, mind if I set them on the window sill?"

"Yeah, just don't ruin my view of the freeway," he said. I was afraid he wasn't kidding.

"So, how are you doing?"

"Okay, I guess. Cops were back yesterday, asking more questions."

"And?"

"And what? You think I'd live out the day if I gave 'em any names? God, I'm just lucky those guys didn't kill me."

"Maybe you should think about another line of work, Freddy."

"Ahhh, not this bullshit again. I already told you I'm a criminal and I'm pretty good at it."

"Really? Gee, could have fooled me."

"Come on, Haskell, like I said before, you and me we're in the same industry, just working different sides of the street. You know?"

127

"Not really. Listen, I think I might have some bad news for you."

"What? They aren't gonna arrest me are they? For getting the shit kicked out of me? Come on, what the hell is the damn charge?"

"No one's arresting you, Freddy or anyone else for that matter, at least as far as I know."

"So what's the problem?"

"Your car?"

"My car? Stay away from that, I busted my ass to get that thing, it's my brand, it's who I am. It makes a statement, God damn it."

"Yeah, and I think it's been stolen."

"What? Stolen? How the hell do you know that?"

"Did you park it at Nasty's?"

"Yeah, right where I always do, back by the dumpsters."

"Well, you may have parked it there, but it's not sitting there now. I just checked."

"Oh Jesus, they, they took my car? What the hell for? Hey, do me a favor, open that closet door, my jeans are hanging on the hook, check the pockets for me."

I pushed the white sliding door to the side and exposed some laminated shelves and four white plastic clothes hangers. There was a white plastic hook attached to the wall that Freddy's jeans and T-shirt hung on. Both looked to be the victims of an assault and in a way I guess they were. They were heavily bloodstained, the jeans especially, since the T-shirt was black, it hid most of the blood that had splashed on it. Both knees were ripped in the jeans.

"See if my keys are in the pocket," Freddy said.

I checked the pockets, one of the back pockets had been ripped open and was barely hanging on. "No, nothing, Freddy."

"God damn it, are you kidding me? Is my wallet in there?"

I shook my head. "No, there's nothing, they're all empty, one of your back pockets is almost torn off."

"Those bastards, wait till I get my car back, I'll kill 'em."

"Well, that's another thing."

"What?" He had a look on his battered face that seemed to ask 'what else could go wrong?'

"Remember how we met, you checking out that house?"

"That place I was checking for Bulldog, where we had the beers?"

"Yeah, that's the place. See, the woman who lived there, the gal who owns the place, she was sitting at a stoplight last night and someone came around the corner, broadsided her and then took off."

"So?"

"Well, she's thought it might have been a black car. I'm thinking Bulldog was driving your car and tried to kill her. For all I know he might be thinking he succeeded."

"God, not my car," Freddy whined completely missing the point that someone, quite possibly Bulldog, had attempted to use the vehicle as a murder weapon.

"I'm just saying it looks that way, Freddy. Can't prove anything yet, but I'm thinking, yeah probably."

"When I get out of here they're gonna pay. Every damn one of them, you hear me, Haskell. I don't care what they did to me, but if they fucked with black beauty they are dead meat."

I didn't doubt him.

Chapter Twenty-Eight

Casey returned my call while I was walking back to my car in the hospital ramp. "Sorry I missed your call, Dev. I left my phone downstairs."

"You sleep okay?"

"Yeah, two bottles of wine will do that."

"I can be over there in about fifteen minutes and drive you back to your place to get the car if that works."

"Can you make it a half-hour, I should jump in the shower first."

"I'll give you forty-five minutes."

I picked her up and we drove over to her house. I walked in with her and headed for the kitchen while she talked with the contractors for a few minutes then came out in the kitchen where I was sitting.

"I put some coffee on, you want some?"

"Yeah," she said then gave a sigh. "I suppose I should get the spare keys out of his desk drawer and get that damn car," she said not sounding at all thrilled with the proposition.

She'd joined a club no one wanted to be a member of; people who'd had their lover torn from them. Whether she realized it or not, she had a year of firsts ahead of her. The first time she was in his car without him. The first time she was at friends' for dinner, the first 4th of July, Labor Day, Halloween on and on and always without him, forever.

"Why don't you get the keys and I'll go out there with you."

She nodded and looked relieved for half a moment then took a deep breath and headed up the stairs to their bedroom.

"Well, here we go," she said a couple minutes later and unlocked the side door of the garage. I was right behind her and pressed the button to raise the double door. "Come on I'll give you a ride to the front," she said then let out a sort of nervous little laugh.

It was vintage Dermot, the car, a dark blue Toyota Camry, about six or seven years old. I walked around to the passenger side and noticed the Obama sticker on the rear bumper. I climbed in and buckled up then waited for about twenty minutes while Casey adjusted the seat.

"Am I being too fickle?" she asked and then moved the seat back again, maybe a quarter-of-an-inch.

"No, no take your time."

She adjusted the rear view mirror, then the side mirrors maybe a half dozen times. "Okay, I think I'm ready."

"God, are you sure?"

"Shut up," she said, but smiled and that seemed to release some more of the pressure. She turned the ignition, then shifted and we jumped ahead into the garage wall.

"The other way might be faster."

She shot me a look, but didn't say anything then put the car in reverse and backed out very slowly. She came to a complete stop every two or three feet. We drove around the block and she parked on the street just behind my car.

"There mission accomplished," she said and turned the car off.

"Good job, Casey. I'm gonna grab some things out of the house then get down to the office."

"Dev, thanks so much, I didn't mean to take up your entire morning, I'm really sorry."

"You didn't take up the entire morning and I was glad to help. Promise me, if you need anything or have any concerns you'll call, okay?"

"I hate to be a pain? You've got a life."

"Yeah, and you're a part of it. You'll call me, promise?"

"Okay, it would probably serve you right anyway," she said then leaned over and gave me a kiss on the cheek. "You're a good guy, Dev."

"Let just keep that our secret," I said and we got out of the car.

I noticed she sort of drifted toward the front of the car before she crossed the street, probably to check for damage after she'd banged into the garage wall. I couldn't see any.

I grabbed a couple of things from the den, the guy from seven-thirty this morning was in there walking around on a pair of stilts touching up the ceiling plaster. He nodded a 'hi' and kept on working. About the only thing I accomplished for the rest of the day was I met Louie at The Spot around five-thirty. He'd apparently been there for a while.

"Good thing you showed up, man. I don't have any cash."

"There's an ATM between the juke box and that pinball machine," I reminded him.

"First of all, I'm not paying four and a half bucks to get my money from that ATM and second, well there might be a problem."

"Don't tell me your card's declined, again."

"Apparently."

"Why?"

"Beats me, I just planned to keep running up a tab, I figured someone I knew was bound to come in sooner or later. And, if that didn't work I'd most likely be drunk enough that it wouldn't matter."

I couldn't fault his logic. We had three drinks total, my beer and two more of Louie's bourbon's. The news came on and Jimmy turned the station to Dancing with the Stars.

"Jimmy, let me settle up with you, I'm getting Louie's, too."

"Thanks," he said. "Its not like we got a lot of dishes he could wash or something he could do to earn his keep."

"Louie, why don't you come home with me? I got beer and I think there's cold pizza in the fridge."

"How long has the pizza been there?" Louie asked.

"Would it make a difference?"

"Now that you mention it, not really."

Chapter Twenty-Nine

I sipped another beer as I half-watched the news with my feet up on the coffee table. The .38 was within easy reach on an end table. Louie was snoring in the chair next to me. I was scrolling through text messages and not really paying attention to what was on when they gave a quick report about a car fire.

To be correct it was a story about a car being set ablaze earlier that morning. They showed the burnt out hulk of the car and the fire crew that was on the scene extinguishing the thing. It had been burning in a seldom used parking lot down along the river. It would be a pretty safe guess the car was most likely stolen and although the front end looked to have been involved in a fairly serious accident even as a burned out hulk, the body bore an awfully close resemblance to Fat Freddy's 'black beauty' Camaro.

I phoned Aaron's office number and left a message. Then I sent a text message to Casey telling her to call me when she got the text. Aaron returned my call around noon the following day.

"Haskell In…"

"You called?"

"Yeah, about sixteen hours ago."

"My deepest apologies, I'm so sorry, but I might just have one or two other things hanging fire down here that take precedence. What the hell did you want?"

"Did you see last night's news?"

"Dev, we all appreciate hearing from concerned citizens such as yourself, but unless someone shot one of the newscasters on the air and no one has reported it yet, what's your point?"

"There was a report about a car set on fire down along the Lilydale road. I'm guessing it was stolen and…."

"And has an identification number that matches the 2014 Z-18 Camaro owned by Mr. Frederick Zimmerman. The license plates had been removed, to answer your next question and no, a quick search of the immediate area did not turn them up."

"Did you search the river around there? You know in the water, some idiot could have just tossed them in there."

"Right now we're dealing with a stolen car that was torched. I'm not calling divers out to search the river bottom for a quarter of a mile in all directions to confirm what we already know."

"I was just thinking."

"Don't, please don't. You are forbidden to think, which shouldn't be too hard for you. You are also forbidden to call me from here on in unless you, yourself have been murdered, in which case you wouldn't be able to call anyway. Then that would allow me to get back to doing what they pay me to do. Goodbye," he said and hung up.

I decided to spread more cheer and drove over to Regions Hospital. I didn't bother to check at the information desk, I just went up to the third floor then navigated the jungle path back to Fat Freddy's room. He was staring out the window when I walked in.

"Hey, Freddy, how's it going?"

"How do you think?" he said. "You ever have to spend some time in this joint? God, I'd rather do a month in the workhouse."

I nodded like I understood.

"By the way, great job on my flowers, look at them."

The flowers I'd set on the windowsill yesterday were pretty much just a half dozen stems in brackish water. There was a pile of petals mounded around the base of the cheap glass vase.

"Didn't exactly get my money's worth, did I?"

"You got screwed is what you got," he said and that thought seemed to cheer him up a little.

"I talked to one of my cop pals this morning."

"Please tell me they shot Bulldog while he tried to escape."

"No such luck. Actually, there was a car that got torched early yesterday morning down along the river. I caught it on the news last night."

"Oh shit, you're kidding me, don't fucking tell me."

"Yeah, it was your black beauty."

"Did you hear what I just said? I said 'don't fucking tell me,' dumb shit."

"You were gonna find out sooner or later, I thought you should know."

"They're sure it's mine?"

"Yeah, they got the vehicle number, I'm afraid it checks out."

"They gonna arrest Bulldog?" he asked.

"No, they really can't, Freddy. There's really no way to even prove he was involved."

"What about fingerprints?"

"The thing was torched and even if they could prove he was somehow in contact with the vehicle it could have been from when he was with you. Didn't you tell me you drove him around once so he could pick up the cash from those little stores?"

"I drove his fat ass around a lot more than once. God, I can't believe they did that, torched my damn car," he said then tears begin to well up in his eyes. He blinked them back and cleared his throat a couple of times.

"Sorry to be the one to tell you, Freddy, but I thought you should know."

He returned to staring out the window.

After a long moment I said, "Hey, I guess I'll be taking off, leave you to your thoughts. I'll see you 'round, Freddy." I turned and headed out the door.

"Haskell," Freddy yelled just as I was about to step into the hallway.

"Yeah, Freddy."

"I'm going to get those guys just as soon as I get out of here," he said.

"You let me know if there's anything I can do for you, Freddy."

He gave me an almost imperceptible nod then went back to staring out the window at the freeway traffic.

__Chapter Thirty__

__Casey called me back__ just as I was getting lunch. "Hang on for a second, Casey," I said, then placed my order. "I'll have two McChickens."

"Would you like anything to drink?"

"No thanks."

"Did you want fries with that?"

"No."

"Your total is two dollars and fourteen cents please pull around to the first window to pay."

"You still there, Casey?"

"Hey sorry, I see you're back on that health food kick. I just saw your text message a minute ago. What's up?"

"Where are you?"

"I'm at the house picking out room colors."

"You gonna be there for a bit?"

"Yeah, I guess. Is everything okay?"

"Yeah, no problems on this end, Casey. Just wanted to check in. I finished early and I'm heading up to your place. I'll be at the house in the next half hour if you're gonna still be there."

"I'll be looking for you," she said and hung up.

On the drive over to Casey's house I was practicing different ways to tell her that I thought the same guy who killed Dermot, namely Bulldog, was trying to kill her. I wasn't coming up with a nice way to say it. On the way I stopped at Solo Vino and picked up a bottle of sparkling white wine thinking that couldn't hurt. I arrived at Casey's a lot sooner than I wanted.

She was talking to two guys in the front parlor while she held color swatches up against the wall. They were nodding in agreement to whatever she'd just said. She turned and gave me a smile as I came in the front door then said, "Give us a couple of minutes, Dev. I'll see you in the kitchen."

That was just fine with me. I walked back to the kitchen, set out two wine glasses, opened the bottle, filled the glasses and tried to practice my lines, it still wasn't working. I heard the front door close and a moment later I heard Casey's footsteps coming through the dining room.

"Oh, Dev, what a surprise, isn't that sweet. You are just so nice. What's the occasion?"

"I think someone's trying to kill you," I blurted out.

She stood there in shock for a long moment just staring at me.

"What?"

"I've been doing some checking, I don't think it was an accident the other night, that guy that broadsided you."

She sort of slumped onto a kitchen stool and just stared at her wine glass with a numb look on her face.

"Let me explain," I said.

She looked at me, but I wasn't sure she actually saw me, she seemed in shock.

"Casey?"

"Dev, if you're trying to be funny that is the most awful thing anyone has ever done to me in my entire life."

"Believe me, I'm not finding anything funny about this."

She closed her eyes and slowly shook her head from side to side.

"You started me thinking when I drove you to your brother's after the accident. You said something about a black car."

"Yeah."

"I heard about a criminal kind of guy who was beaten up and robbed. Whoever did it put him in the hospital."

She had a look on her face like this wasn't making any sense, but didn't say anything.

"Anyway, his car was stolen. I'm pretty sure, well in fact I know it's the same car that was driving past your house that night you called me."

"The same car?"

"Yeah. He was assaulted, his car was stolen and then it was found torched down along the river early yesterday morning. The thing had been in an accident. I think whoever stole his car was following you, cut through that parking lot and came around and broadsided you. The fact that you jumped the car forward most likely saved your life. Then the driver took off and well, torched the car to destroy any of the evidence."

"And you know this for certain?" she said then gulped down about half her glass of wine.

"I know the same guy who was creeping you out the night you first called me was assaulted and had his car stolen. I know that car was involved in an accident and I know the same car was set on fire down along the river."

"Did you tell the police?"

"Actually they told me about the car, they confirmed it by the vehicle id number."

"And who owns it," she shook her head suggesting things weren't making sense then gulped more wine like that might help.

"Well, I sort of know the guy, know of him I guess."

"And he was assaulted, you said?"

"Yeah, he's in Regions right now. He's gonna be okay, I went and visited him and…"

"What?" she screamed.

"He's in Regions, they beat him up pretty bad so he'll probably be there for a couple more days."

"You went and visited him? This, this maniac who was stalking me. Is he the bastard who shot Dermot?" she screamed.

"No Casey, he didn't have anything to do with that, I don't think."

"You don't think, Dev, Dermot is dead, he's not coming back. Do you know that? Do you even fucking understand? Does anyone? He is not coming back. He is not going to walk in that door and kiss me tonight. I'll never hear him laugh, ever again. He is not coming back," she said then a tear rolled down her cheek and she started to cry.

I let her sit there and cry for a long moment, hoping she'd just get it out of her system. I wanted to hold her, but I didn't think she'd accept that just now. Finally I said, "I know all that, Casey. God, do I ever know it. I'm trying to find out who is responsible. I'm trying to help the cops. I've been in touch with them every day and they, or rather we, are doing everything we possibly can to find who is responsible. And when we find them and we will, they'll be arrested."

She raised her head up slowly and looked at me, then rubbed her hand under her nose and sniffled. "Arrested? You're going to have them arrested?"

"Casey, look, I'm telling you all this because you are in danger, too. I don't know why. I don't know what caused any of this, but I'm trying and the police are trying. We're all working very hard to find out what in the hell is going on. Right now, the most important thing we can do is get you in a safe place."

"I'm at Tommy's."

"That's right and the other night you thought you were being followed."

"But the car turned?"

"I think he went through the parking lot, circled the building and smashed into your car. You can't stay at Tommy's. We need to get you out of town, the sooner the better."

"But the house?" she said and sort of looked around.

"The house will be fine. I'll stay here, right now I'm worried about you. You have somewhere you could go, someplace out of town?"

"Ahhh, a girlfriend in Chicago, but I think she's out of town now. Umm, an old collage roommate down in New Orleans, I guess."

"Can you call her?"

"Yeah, I suppose I can, but?"

"Call her, tell her you got a chance to get away and you want to visit. You got cash?"

"A little, but, Dev, this is crazy."

"Look, I'll buy the ticket, you call her, now. I'm calling the airline maybe there's something out of here yet today."

142

"Today?"

"Call her, Casey," I said and pulled my cell out to call the airline. It turned out there was a 7:30pm flight to Atlanta and then a hop to New Orleans. Eight hundred bucks and it wasn't even direct. Casey was on the phone to her former roommate.

"I know it just sort of happened all of a sudden," she was saying into her phone as she looked over at me.

I nodded and said, "You'll get in at 12:30am, I'm booking it now."

Chapter Thirty-One

"I don't know, I still think this is just crazy," Casey said.

I was about to merge into the main terminal entrance. We'd just passed the sign on the freeway that always said there was an amber alert and to contact authorities if you saw any suspicious activity. It was five o'clock, peak rush hour, but we were still a good twenty minutes ahead of schedule.

"You left Tommy a note?" I asked.

"Yeah, and I'll call him as soon as I get through security."

"Just tell him you're going on a whim and you needed to get out of town."

"They'll probably be glad to see me go. You know how it is with a houseguest after a few days."

"I'll keep you posted, call me whenever and as often as you like. You think of anything, Casey no matter how insignificant it might seem you call me."

"Okay, okay," she said as I pulled into the departure drop off area in front of the Delta door.

"You stay safe down there, and just relax. You need anything communicated to the contractor just let me know and I…"

"I've got his number, Dev," she said and opened the car door. She pulled her suitcase out of the back seat and set it on the curb. She closed the rear door then leaned back into the front seat and stared at me for a long moment. "Sorry if I yelled earlier. I know you're just trying to keep me safe. Just one more thing,"

"Sure, you name it, Casey."

"That arrest. It doesn't work for me, Dev. I want that bastard killed. It's what he did to Dermot, it's what he deserves."

Casey, I don't think…"

"I am so not kidding. I want that bastard killed, Dev. I don't want him arrested. I don't want him to go to trial. I want him to be dead. He doesn't deserve to live. Dead. Promise me." She said and then just stared at me with very cold eyes.

"I'll see what I can do, Casey."

"I'm not fucking around, Dev," she said very softly, leaving no doubt, then she slammed the car door and stormed into the airport.

Chapter Thirty-Two

I had nightmares throughout the night. I couldn't really remember what any of them were about and maybe that's a good thing. I woke well before the work crew arrived and decided to just get up and get dressed. I was drinking coffee in the kitchen when they arrived. I was seated at the kitchen counter reading the text message from Casey that came through last night letting me know she'd arrived safe and sound.

I left the house a little after eight and took a detour on the way to my office stopping in at Regions Hospital. The couple of times I'd been there made the path back to Freddy's room seem not so convoluted. I walked past the nurse's station and into his room with a wise guy greeting on the tip of my tongue. The room was empty, the cheap glass vase on the window sill was gone, the bed was stripped and Freddy was nowhere to be found.

I went out to the nurse's station. A man and a woman were seated behind the counter in blue hospital scrubs. Both of them held clipboards on their laps and had stethoscopes wrapped around their necks.

"Hi, what can I do for you?" the guy said to me.

"I'm looking for Freddy Zimmerman, it looks like he's been moved to another room."

"Oh no, sorry," the woman said. "Mr. Zimmerman checked himself out very early this morning."

"Checked himself out? Was he okay to go?"

"We didn't think so," she said. "But we can't force people to stay. He wanted to leave, so he left."

"What time was this?"

"Just a little after three."

"A little after three? In the morning?"

She nodded and said, "Yup."

"Is that normal?"

"Nothing's really normal on this wing. He was dressed, told us he was leaving and then just walked out."

"Do you know where he went?"

"Down that hall," she said then pointed and smiled.

I glanced down the hall at the wheeled cart with a number of breakfast trays stacked on it. A woman dressed in white was carrying one of the trays into a room. The tile floors were so highly polished you could watch her mirror-like reflection as it drifted out of sight.

"Was there anything else, sir?"

"No, thanks for the update," I said and walked down the hall.

I'd been back in the office accomplishing absolutely nothing when Louie waltzed in. "You got the coffee on?"

"It's about the only positive thing I've accomplished in the past twenty-four hours."

"That's better than some days," he said then went over and poured himself a cup. He settled into his chair, took a sip then studied me.

"Heidi dump you again?" he asked.

"No, she didn't dump me, and for your information we're not even in a relationship. Well, the occasional get together, but we're free to date other people."

"Okay, so what's up?"

I went over and poured myself a fresh cup of coffee then proceeded to bring Louie up to speed. I told him about Casey's accident, Freddy's car, Casey fleeing the saintly city and Freddy disappearing.

"Man, you have managed to screw up a number of people's lives in a very short amount of time."

"Me? I'm just helping out."

"Yeah, sure that's what you've been doing. Just a thought here, Dev. Do you remember your visit to Jackie Van Dorn where you end up assaulting your new best friend, Fat Freddy? Then, you told the bouncer's at Nasty's that Freddy was supposed to let them know Bulldog and Tubby had sent you over to mind Swindle Lawless. You questioned Swindle about Bulldog. I don't know, just a wild guess here, but do you think some wigged out psychopath like Bulldog or even Tubby for that matter might start putting two and two together and take matters into their own hands? Maybe try and beat someone half to death or kill them with a stolen car?"

"You make it sound like everything that happened is my fault."

"Well?"

"What do you mean, well? What did I do?"

"When you look at it from another point of view, I'd say you've done just about everything you shouldn't have done. That assault on Fat Freddy, think that might have been a message to you?"

"A message? To me?"

"Then the hit and run."

He had me thinking.

"Sounds like the one bright thing you've done was to get that girl out of town. What did your friend Lieutenant LaZelle have to say?"

"He told me not to call him again unless I'd been murdered, in which case I wouldn't be able to call and he could get on with his work."

Louie smiled and said, "Maybe follow his advice."

Chapter Thirty-Three

I was pondering my next move later that night in front of the flat screen. I was only half watching the movie about wives getting revenge on their cheating husbands. It was supposed to be a comedy, but I wasn't in the laughing mood. I'd already forgotten the title and didn't seem to have the energy to push the off button on the remote. It was close to midnight and I had most of the lights turned on throughout the first floor of Casey's house. I was drinking a beer and my .38 was sitting on the end table, nestled in between the four bottles I'd already finished.

At first I thought it might have been the radiators then realized it was summer and the heat wasn't on. I heard the noise again, a sort of soft knock coming from the kitchen area. I set my beer down, grabbed the .38 and walked to the back of the house. I turned off the dining room light and then the kitchen light so I would be entering a dark room. I let my eyes adjust for a moment then slowly crouched down and moved along the kitchen counter.

I heard the noise again, it definitely sounded like a knock on the back door. I peaked around the side of the kitchen counter out through the window. There was a fairly large guy out there, slightly illuminated by the new motion detector lights attached to the side of the house. His back was to me and he seemed to be twitching and glancing around nervously. He turned, put his hands up against the kitchen window and tried to peer into the darkened room. Fat Freddy.

I watched him for a long moment. Long enough that the motion detector light went off and he just stood out there in the dark. He seemed to be alone. When Freddy stopped looking in the kitchen window I moved toward the back door.

"What do you want?" I said through the closed door. I was standing off to the side and still crouched just in case he started shooting.

"Haskell? Jesus Christ, open the damn door and let me in, I'm getting eaten alive out here."

"What do you want?"

"Will you, come on for Christ sake, ouch, damn it. God these things are going crazy, come on man, open up."

I opened the door, stepped back and trained the .38 on Freddy nose. "Get in here and close the door behind you."

"God, it's about damn time, I was, oh what the hell, put that damn thing away," he said and closed the door behind him. I could suddenly hear the high pitch of mosquito's as they swarmed in with him.

"Where's the damn light switch," he said and started moving one of his paws up and down along the wall. He found the switch and turned on the light. His face was partially hidden by the splint on his nose. He was dressed in the jeans and T-shirt I'd seen hanging in his hospital room. Both pieces of clothing were caked with blood and the legs of his jeans had been torn off where the knees had ripped making a rather odd pair of shorts. One leg on the shorts extended about three inches longer than the other.

"You got something to eat, man. I've been walking and haven't had a thing all day."

"What the hell are you doing, Freddy? Why in God's name did you leave the hospital?" I said then flipped on the light in the kitchen. "Come on, we'll see what I've got to eat."

Freddy settled onto one of the kitchen stools and I heard the thing creak as his weight oozed across the seat. "How 'bout a beer for starters?" I said opening the refrigerator.

"Now you're talking," he replied.

I took two beers out of the fridge, a pizza delivery box and then a white Styrofoam container that I think Heidi had left about a week ago. I opened the beers and slid one across the plywood topped counter to Freddy. He had already dug into the pizza box and was in the process of inhaling a very large piece. I opened the Styrofoam container, took one look and tossed the thing into the trash. I turned on the oven, took two frozen pizzas out of the freezer and began to unwrap them. "Soon as that oven heats up, I'll toss these in."

Freddy nodded and attacked another piece out of the delivery box.

"So, you checked yourself out of Regions."

"Had to, man," he said then stuffed the better part of an entire piece in his mouth and chewed.

"At three in the morning?"

"How'd you know that?" he said then wiped his hands back and forth across his disgustingly filthy T-Shirt.

"I went down there to check on you, one of the nurses told me."

"The blonde with that little tattoo?"

152

"She was blonde, but I didn't notice any tattoo."

"Little heart thing on her wrist. Not much of one, I mean why even bother if that's all you're getting?"

"You checked yourself out," I said getting back on track.

"Yeah, I'm lying there, asleep in my room and suddenly someone's shaking my shoulder. I'm thinking it's one of those nurses, you know how they wake you up and check your blood pressure and shit? Sometimes I think they were just doing it to mess me up."

I nodded like it would be perfectly logical for a nurse to come around in the middle of the night to mess a patient up.

"So, I'm opening my eyes, coming awake and all of a sudden this hand goes over my mouth, it kinda tasted like barbeque sauce, course it's that butthead, Dallas."

"Dallas?"

"He's one of the bouncers at Nasty's. He's the same jerk that sucker punched me in the parking lot, then once I was down the rest of those twats came out of nowhere and it was open season on your boy."

"He was in your hospital room?"

"Yeah, way past visiting hours by the way, I mean it was after midnight. Anyway, the jerk puts his grimy hand over my mouth then said he's got a little something for me and tosses my car keys on the table. Kind of laughs then tells me thanks for the ride."

"He says that, 'thanks for the ride'?"

"That ain't all," Freddy said, then grabbed the last slice of pizza out of the delivery box. "He says, you know what's good for you, you won't be talking to the cops. We hear anything and you're dead."

"That doesn't sound too promising."

"You're telling me," he said then rolled the pizza slice up and stuffed the entire thing into his mouth.

"What are you going to do?"

He pointed to his mouth, his cheeks looked like a chipmunk storing nuts, bulging while he attempted to chew. Finally he said, "Hey, those dudes fucked with black beauty, that ain't on, man. It was my statement, who I was."

"Your brand," I added.

"Exactly, man, I just can't have it. Hey, you gonna put those other two pizzas in?"

Chapter Thirty-Four

Freddy slept in the same chair Louie had crashed in the other night. He said he didn't feel safe going back to his apartment and I sure didn't feel like driving him anywhere, so he spent the night.

I shook him awake before the work crew arrived and had him take a much needed shower. None of Dermot's clothes and certainly none of mine were going to fit him so I drove him over to Menard's, a DIY and construction store that carried everything from paint to lumber and plumbing supplies. They also carried some basic articles of clothing like jeans and shirts. We walked out of there with a pair of jeans, socks, boxers and a half dozen T-shirts for under forty bucks.

"Can't thank you enough for helping me out, Dev. Kinda like that movie, you know."

"What movie's that?"

"The Grandfather."

"The grand..., you mean the Godfather?"

"Yeah, I think that's the one."

"Look, Freddy, you're going to need some wheels if you plan to get back on your feet. I've got access to another car for a couple of days. You could use this one maybe till the end of the week if that would help you out."

He sort of snickered then said, "That's righteous, man. No offense, Dev, but whatever your driving here isn't exactly the sort of statement I want to make."

"It's a Saturn Ion, 2003," I bragged. With Fat Freddy in the front seat the car was pulling decidedly to the right and the engine seemed to groan every time I attempted to accelerate.

"I'm just hoping no one I know sees me in this thing, I've got a reputation, you know."

"Yeah about that, Freddy, your rep. I'm thinking it might not be a bad idea to lay a little low for awhile."

"We'll see, I got some things cooking," Freddy said then gazed out the window signaling the conversation wasn't going to go much further.

"Well, you better come up with some sort of alternative plan. They fired you from Nasty's, so you're gonna need a job. You don't have a vehicle and you're afraid to go back to your apartment. What else am I missing?"

"I think there's a warrant or two out for my arrest?"

"A warrant or two?"

"Just a misunderstanding, well and a bunch of parking tickets."

"What's the misunderstanding?"

"Some petty kind of bullshit about me assaulting a guy, it's nothing."

"Assaulting a guy?"

"My landlord. I didn't know it at the time, but that worthless piece of shit turns out to be some sort of shirt-tail relative of someone in the City Attorney's office. Makes the guy think he can jack me around. I sort of fell behind just a little on my rent."

156

"How little?"

"Only a couple of months, I told that asshole I was good for it, but he wouldn't listen, which really pissed me off. Then, when he pad locked the door to my apartment I'd had it and went downstairs to educate the man."

"And did you?"

"Yeah, but at the time I didn't know there were witnesses. Anyway, that's sort of another reason I can't go back to my place, the cops are probably looking for me."

"So, if for some reason you get stopped by the police, they're most likely going to haul you in."

"Well, yeah, but I don't plan on being stopped."

"There you go then, problem solved."

Freddy nodded.

I dropped him off back at Casey's house to watch TV while I went down to the office. I got a text from Casey around noon; 'All well here, having a great time'.

I replied with; 'All well up here, stay safe.' Then held my breath in the event she was on one of her texting benders, thankfully she didn't reply.

I was back at Casey's house towards the end of the day. The contractors had all left and Freddy greeted me with a loud belch then said, "Hey, you're out of beer and pizza, man." Once he made that statement he returned to watching some sort of reality show.

I went back out the door and purchased those two necessities. I tossed two of the pizzas I'd purchased into the oven and called Freddy twenty minutes later. It was like calling a puppy, "Freddy, dinner, Freddy."

He waddled into the kitchen a moment later smiling and wearing his new jeans. He'd taken the metal splint off his nose, but there were still traces of adhesive on his cheeks. His nose didn't look all that great. It was sort of a pasty gray color where it wasn't still black and blue and had taken on a sort of sagging shape like it was considering just falling off his face.

I had three slices of pizza for dinner, Freddy ate the remaining six slices from that pizza then devoured the entire second pizza all by himself.

"Mmm-mmm, really good man. You got any ice cream?"

"I think there's some in the freezer, check it out," I said and nodded toward the refrigerator.

Freddy slid off his stool, pulled the bottom freezer drawer open and studied the contents. "You got a preference, looks like vanilla or some butter pecan shit."

"I'll take a pass, none for me," I said.

"Suit yourself," he said, then grabbed one of the containers out of the drawer. He took a spoon from the silverware tray and sat back down. He tore the lid off and proceeded to eat directly out of the ice cream container. "Hey, man, think you could give me a lift later tonight?"

"Yeah, I suppose, as long as it's not too late."

"I'm thinking around ten, is that too late?"

"We going far?"

"No, maybe five, six minutes away is all. I won't need a ride back."

"Yeah, I can do that," I said.

"Thanks, man, I think I'm gonna relax and catch some tube," he said then walked into the den with the ice cream.

Freddy called from the den a couple of hours later. "Dev, can you still give me a lift?"

I'd been sitting at the kitchen counter and had just sent an email to Casey telling her everything was okay and to relax and enjoy the Big Easy.

"Yeah, sure, let me just grab my keys," I said, then logged off and headed out the front door.

Freddy was waiting for me on the porch with a baseball bat.

"What's with that?" I asked.

"Got a pal on a softball team, he plays for his church, they got some league competition or something this weekend. He wanted to borrow my bat so I told him I'd get it over to him."

Chapter Thirty-Five

I wasn't sure why we had to get Freddy's softball bat over to his pal this late at night, but on the other hand if it got Freddy out of the house it was worth the effort. The ride over to his pal's house was more like fifteen minutes and other than the occasional direction Freddy wasn't talking.

"That's it up there," he finally said as I came round the corner. "Just drop me off behind that pickup parked on the street, that'll be perfect."

I pulled up behind a large black pickup truck. It sported one of those rebel flag rear window graphic things. Giant chrome-lined mud flaps with the silhouette of a naked woman hung behind the large, dual rear tires. Chrome letters spelled out F-350 4x4 across the rear. A black and white bumper sticker read 'Protected by Smith and Wesson'.

"God, sweet ride, that baby's a Diesel V8. It'll blow anyone away in seconds," Freddy said

We were in the Midway district of St. Paul and the homes up and down the block looked to have been built in the 1920's. The pickup was parked in front of one of the less-attractive structures on the street. A story-and-a-half wood frame house with peeling-white clapboard siding, faded green trim, a dilapidated front porch and a sagging roof. There was an old upholstered couch sitting on the porch that looked like it had been through one too many rain storms. A dim light drifted out from the front room and through the window you could see a TV was on.

"Thanks, Dev, not sure when I'll be back. Appreciate all you've done, you've been a big help."

"Not a problem, Freddy, give me a call tomorrow if you need a lift."

Freddy smiled and climbed out, then closed the door and gave a quick wave as he walked across the small front yard and up the steps. He rang the doorbell then turned and faced me. I waited for a pair of headlights approaching in my side mirror to pass by before I pulled away from the curb. As the car drove past I gave a quick glance back at Freddy.

A large guy with a shaved head and a snarl on his face was just opening the front door. I watched as Freddy stabbed the end of the baseball bat into the guy's solar plexus then grabbed him by his T-shirt and yanked him out onto the porch. He slammed the bat up into the guys chin causing his head to snap back. The poor bastard attempted to raise his arms in a sort of defensive position, but Freddy wound up and gave a low, full force swing into the guy's knee with the bat.

I couldn't hear the crack, but it looked like the knee completely snapped. He half rolled and attempted to crawl off the porch as Freddy stepped over him and with all his three-hundred-and-fifty-plus pounds stomped on the guy's back then held him in place with his foot. He slammed the bat into the guy's right hand then adjusted his swing and nailed the left hand to the porch floor. As the guy lifted his head to scream Freddy kicked him so hard in the side of the head that he rolled over.

I was in the process of getting out of my car as Freddy reached down and tore the front pocket of the guy's shorts open, then stood up and triumphantly brandished a set of keys. He stepped over the motionless figure lying on the porch floor and walked back toward me. The entire assault couldn't have taken more than fifteen seconds.

"What the hell do you think your doing? Are you insane?"

"Meet Dallas," Freddy said thrusting a thumb over his shoulder. He hurried past me and tossed the baseball bat into the back of the pickup truck. "I told you, once they screwed with black beauty they were gonna pay."

"But, Jesus Christ, did you kill him?"

"No, unfortunately, but he ain't gonna be chasing me or anyone else for that matter, probably ever again. Appreciate you doing this for me, Dev. I'll be in touch," he said then pushed a button on the keys and the pickup's lights blinked. "Always nice talking to you, Dallas," he called, then climbed into the pickup and drove away.

I started across the lawn toward the figure lying halfway down the front steps. Suddenly the porch light came on next door, curtains on a side window twitched as a woman stared out and the front door began to open. I panicked and hurried back into my car and quickly pulled away with my lights off. I screeched around the first right turn, flicked on my lights and slowed down. I took the long way back to Casey's and constantly checked for someone following me, I never spotted anyone.

I parked in Casey's garage then hurried to the back door, looking left and right across her backyard with every other step. I quickly closed the door behind me, locked it then proceeded to turn all the lights on throughout the first floor. I double checked to make sure both the front and back doors were locked then pulled a bottle of Jameson down from the cupboard and poured a healthy amount into a glass. I didn't waste any time getting an ice cube.

I drifted off to sleep well after midnight, or did I just pass out? The following morning I was aware of the contractors working for a good while before I crawled off the couch. The Jameson bottle was empty and lay on its side underneath the coffee table. My empty glass sat on the end table next to the .38. The ceiling light and both lamps were still on in the den. I tucked the .38 in my belt, pulled my T-shirt out to cover the gun and made my way to the bathroom.

Even though it was a cloudy day I was wearing sunglasses on my way to work. I bought a newspaper from the machine on the corner then climbed upstairs to the office. Louie was at his desk.

"Out till the wee hours were we?" Louie asked as I threw the newspaper on my desk and made my way to the coffee pot.

"No, I never left the house. Stayed in all night doing some research on the internet," I said, then hurried back to my desk without looking at him.

I opened the paper and read the headlines on the front page then quickly paged through the entire paper, scanning page after page looking for an assault report or worse, a murder. I couldn't find anything.

I was aware Louie would look up and study me from time to time, then go back to the files spread out across his picnic table. Finally he said, "Dev, is everything all right?"

"Yeah, sure, just fine. Why?"

"I don't know you just seem, sort of jumpy or something."

"No, no, everything's just fine. No problems."

"You're sure."

"Yeah, I'm sure.

"Okay, 'cause if there was something wrong you could tell me, you know."

"Louie, relax everything's fine, just thinking some stuff through is all, no problem."

"Okay. Casey all right?"

"Yeah, I've gotten a couple of text messages from her, sounds great. I sent her an email late last night, told her to have a good time and just relax. I can only hope she'll take that advice to heart."

Louie nodded and studied me for a long moment then said, "I'm sure she will."

I'd calmed down by mid-afternoon. I was taking my time driving home and listening to the news reports on a couple of different stations. I didn't pick up anything regarding Freddy's assault on Dallas. It looked like we were in the clear.

Chapter Thirty-Six

"Haskell Investigations," I said. I was fumbling with the backdoor key trying to get it into the lock while at the same time juggling a new bottle of Jameson and my cellphone.

The audible snap of a wad of gum coming through my phone launched my heart up into my throat. "Haskell, Detective Manning, how are you?"

"Just fine, thanks," I said, then got the door unlocked and stepped inside. I locked the door again as soon as it closed then glanced out the window just to make sure Manning wasn't lurking in the bushes.

"Say, your name came up this afternoon," Manning said.

"Was the chief suggesting me as your replacement?"

"Don't get your hopes up. No, seems there was a spot of trouble last night over in the Midway district, an assault, pretty brutal."

"Sorry to disappoint, Detective, but I wouldn't know a thing about something like that. As a matter of fact, I was home all night working on my computer. I think I was online until close to ten, sent a final email off then I had a nightcap and crawled into bed."

"Amazing, you sound like the picture of responsibility."

"That would be me."

"You sent that email on your computer I suppose."

"No, Manning, I used smoke signals, it's so much more fun. Yeah, I sent it on my computer." I was thinking tech probably wasn't Manning's strong suit.

"What OS are you on?" he asked.

"OS?" I thought he was making a joke about some new kind of street drug.

"OS, it stands for operating system, Haskell it's the working brains of your computer. What is it Windows XP? God it couldn't be, probably more like 7, 8 or 8.1."

"I'm not sure."

"You a MAC guy, MAC 10 ring any bells?"

"I don't actually know. To tell you the truth, I just turn the thing on and most of the time it works."

"And you were on last night around ten?"

"Yeah, I was looking at some stuff then sent an email to a friend down in New Orleans."

"I wonder if you'd consider bringing that in here so we could maybe take a look."

"Take a look at my computer?"

"Yes, it wouldn't take us but a couple of minutes to verify the time of your activity and then you could be on your way."

"I suppose, if you really want me to, what time would you like me down there?"

"Actually, Haskell, if you're willing to come in, I'm not really interested in seeing you."

"Okay, anything else?"

"No unfortunately, can't thank you enough for your time," he said then snapped his wad of gum and hung up.

I closed my eyes, took a deep breath and was convinced he knew I was involved in Fat Freddy's assault on Dallas. Those nosey neighbors probably took down my license number, or maybe Freddy just called in an anonymous tip.

I fell asleep in front of the flat screen and woke up thinking I heard the workmen whispering out in the hallway, but it was still dark outside. Then an unpleasantly familiar voice snarled, "Let's check upstairs, that bastards probably passed out in bed with some cheap slut." The unmistakable voice of Bulldog trailed off as a number of feet cautiously tiptoed up the staircase. I heard them enter the room over head, a moment later the footsteps headed back down the hall going from room to room, looking for me. They were no longer tiptoeing and Bulldog was screaming, "Haskell, Haskell, where the hell are you?"

I grabbed the .38 from the end table then tore open my suitcase, pulled out a .45 and quietly stepped out of the den. I was barefoot and wearing a pair of cutoff gray sweatpants.

They came clomping back down the stairs a moment later, three of them. The guy in the front of the pack said, "He's probably out getting laid somewhere." I recognized the tribal tattoos wrapped around his massive biceps. He was the bouncer from Nasty's that had hassled me the other night when I was trying to get Swindle to make some sense.

Bulldog said, "I got some things to take care of upstairs, you two…"

"That's far enough, stop right there," I shouted and flipped on the light.

They looked shocked for half a second before Mr. Tribal Tattoo half jumped down three or four steps to the landing. I fired the .38 at him then pointed the .45

up at the other two. "Go ahead, just give me a reason, Bulldog. I'll kill you, I swear to God."

Both of them spread their hands out in surrender and Bulldog said, "Now just hold on there, Haskell. Take it easy, we just wanted to talk to you, try and find out where Fat Freddy is."

The guy on the landing was rolling back and forth, holding his knee and groaning. "Yeah, sure that's what you were going to do, just talk. I've seen you do that before, I'm not interested. Now listen up, Lowell, I want you to take that piece out of your belt with your left hand, carefully, and then drop it over the railing. Hold it between your finger and thumb."

Bulldog wasn't used to being told what to do and his eyes seemed to flare when I called him Lowell. He half shouted, "Now you just hold on a God damn minute."

I cocked the hammer back on the .45. "You got about three seconds and then I'm gonna blow what little brains you got all over that wall behind you and I'll get a medal from the city for doing it."

He hesitated, maybe trying to read me.

"Three. Two."

"Alright, just calm down, I'm doing it, I'm doing it, damn it, I'm doing it," he said then carefully pulled the pistol out of his belt using just his thumb and forefinger. He dropped it over the railing to the hallway floor below. It landed with a thunk then slid a couple of feet.

"You next," I said to the other idiot on the stairs.

"I don't have a gun," he said.

My eyes glared and I shoved the .45 in his direction.

"Honest, I don't have a gun, please don't shoot, please," he cried out.

The guy with the tribal tattoos groaned and let out a loud cry, "God, my knee why'd you have to do that, God."

"Get him out of here," I said and waved at them with the .45 to move down the stairs. They hurried down and picked the groaner up by the arms. "Get him out of here, I see either one of you around here again, ever, I'm gonna shoot first."

Bulldog looked like he was going to say something then thought better of it. They helped the other fool hobble on one leg out the door. I slammed it shut behind them, clicked the lock then dropped to my knees and threw up.

Chapter Thirty-Seven

I couldn't go back to sleep. By the time I cleaned up the front entry, screwed the window back in place that they'd forced open and put some coffee on, the sun was almost ready to come up. I wandered upstairs with the coffee, wondering what it was Bulldog was referring to when he said he had 'something to take care of upstairs.' I went into each of the bedrooms and stared for a few moments, but nothing jumped out at me.

Maybe he planned to set a fire, or turn the faucets on in the bathroom and plug the drain. Maybe he planned to steal some furniture although that didn't seem likely and God bless Dermot and Casey, but they didn't have the sort of furniture a guy like Bulldog would spend much effort stealing.

I went back through the rooms this time looking under beds, behind chests of drawers. I pulled the mirrors off the walls. The only thing I found was behind the mirror in the master bedroom 'I love you' was penciled on the wall in Dermot's handwriting.

There was an entrance to the attic in the hallway ceiling. A panel that you pushed up into the attic then climbed in. I hauled a stepladder from the front parlor back upstairs. I climbed the ladder then pushed the panel into the attic and popped my head in, it smelled of dust with just a hint of pine. The vast space was empty except for a few boxes stacked against a wall. Even in the early morning the temperature was about fifteen degrees warmer up here.

I pulled myself up into the attic and walked over to investigate the boxes. Unless Bulldog had been interested in a wedding dress, outdated college text books or an empty antique steamer trunk there was nothing there. I lowered myself back onto the ladder and replaced the access panel in the ceiling.

I don't know why exactly, but I remembered Heidi obsessing over that cabinet in the closet off the back bedroom and taking a bunch of pictures. She'd referred to the room as the servants' quarters, or something and said the closet was probably a rear staircase originally. My mind had been on other things at the time.

I went into the closet and stood in front of the cabinet. I couldn't tell much about it except that it was oak and covered most of the wall. I knocked on the wall like Heidi had done, it definitely sounded hollow behind the thing. I pulled an empty drawer out, and examined the bottom for a note or a treasure map or something. I set the drawer on the floor and went through the same process with the other three and didn't find a thing. I went to put the drawers back in when I noticed a panel in the back of the cabinet. It was about two feet square with a long brass ridge along the right side, indicating the back of a hinge.

I pushed the panel hoping it would spring open, but nothing happened. I pulled my car keys out and slid the little bottle opener I have into the space on the left hand side of the panel then pried the thing open. The panel moved maybe an inch and I reached in and swung it open. There was a blue nylon bag with handles in there, bigger than a gym bag, maybe more like something for hockey equipment or to put soccer balls in. It was heavy and I had to use both hands to pull it out. It tumbled to the floor of the cabinet with a loud thunk then I dragged it out onto the closet floor and pulled the zipper back.

There was a pistol in there, an automatic with black cross-hatched grips. It had a clip inserted and I figured it was loaded. It sat on top of a large pile of cash. A very large pile.

I heard a noise down stairs and immediately thought of Bulldog coming back with reinforcements. I zipped the bag closed, pulled the .38 out of my pocket and sat very still. Eventually, I recognized the voices as two of the contractors. I replaced the drawers in the cabinet, stuffed the .38 back in my pocket and carried the bag downstairs to the den. I quickly changed, went out to my car in the garage and locked the bag in the trunk, then drove to my office. I took a round about way, checking the rear view mirror every five seconds or so to see if I was being followed. I never spotted anyone.

When I got to the office it was empty, I figured Louie wouldn't be in for at least a couple more hours. I locked the door then took a chair and wedged it under the doorknob as an added precaution. I looked out the window and studied the street, but didn't see anything out of the ordinary. There was still a half-cup of coffee left in the coffee pot and the thing had apparently been on all night. I dumped the sludge down the drain, let the pot cool for a couple of minutes then made a fresh pot.

I sat at my desk sipping coffee, looking at the nylon bag and occasionally scanning the street. Everything seemed to be in order outside. I unzipped the bag and looked at the pistol lying on top. It seemed a pretty safe bet that the money was due to some sort of criminal enterprise and that the pistol had a better than even chance of being related to some sort of crime. Probably a number of crimes if Bulldog was involved and I had no doubt he was.

I thought about Casey and I thought about Dermot. The reason for Casey's life being torn apart, the reason for Dermot's murder was on my desk. If the money was the result of some criminal enterprise it was also the cause of Dermot's murder. I couldn't prove it yet, but everything seemed to point to Bulldog deciding he would just kill whoever was in his way. But, what he hadn't counted on was two people being home that night and when Casey began screaming he just ran off into the dark.

I fished a pencil out of my desk drawer and slipped it through the trigger housing of the pistol. I carried the pistol dangling from the pencil over to the file cabinet and opened a briefcase I've never used. I set the pistol and the pencil in the briefcase, then closed it and put it back behind the file cabinet.

I started stacking the piles of cash on my desk. They were used bills, all twenties. Each was banded with a homemade paper band, '$5000' was written on the band along with a date, '9/14/11' and then what looked like someone's initials. I emptied the bag and counted the pile on my desk, twice. There were a hundred bundles at five-grand each which made five-hundred grand. I punched the number into my calculator just to double check. Five-hundred grand, a half-a-million bucks and Bulldog had proven he would do anything to get his hands on it again.

The knob turned and the office door thumped a couple of times. Then the knob turned again and I heard

Louie groan, "What the hell?" from the far side of the door.

"Louie?" I called, and began shoveling the bundles back into the bag as fast as I could.

"Yeah, Dev? What's with the door?"

"I'll be there in a second, just finishing up here," I called and shoveled a little faster.

"You okay, Dev? Anything wrong?"

"Nope, no everything is just fine," I said then zipped the bag closed, dropped it on the floor next to my desk and hurried to the door.

"Well then, what the hell...." I pulled the chair out from under the door knob and opened the door. "...are you doing in there?" Louie said and then stood there looking at me.

"I just wanted some private time and didn't expect to see you here so early." I said.

Louie looked at the chair in my hand and said, "I never realized we had a problem with all sorts of people dropping in unannounced."

"I didn't want to be interrupted."

"You hiding some woman in here?" he said then brushed past me, threw his computer bag on the picnic table and charged over to the coffeepot. He filled his mug, took a sip, dribbled on his shirt then settled into his chair. I saw his eyes register on the blue nylon bag, but he didn't say anything.

I went over to my desk, wrote down the date 9/14/11 then picked up the binoculars and pretended to scan the building across the street. I could feel Louie's eyes staring at my back.

I held the binoculars up, but I wasn't looking at anything in particular. In fact they were trained on a tree in the backyard on the corner. I was thinking of the conversation I had in Aaron's office the morning I showed up with the caramel rolls. He was telling me about the disappearance of 'Georgie Boy' Marcela a few months before Bulldog was sentenced.

"Maybe three months before Bulldog gets sentenced Marcela disappears. There've been rumors we pick up from time to time that he skipped town and now he's in Vegas, LA, maybe Miami, someplace like that, but we never hear anything concrete. When he supposedly skipped town he apparently took a lot of cash with him, close to half a million dollars."

I was pretty sure I'd found Georgie Boy's half million bucks. I doubted I or anyone else would ever find Georgie Boy and it was a safe bet he wasn't in Vegas, LA or Miami. It all made sense in some weird way, Bulldog hides the money, goes to jail and his house is sold while he's locked up. Two innocents buy the place and Dermot ends up paying the ultimate price.

Louie made a couple of phone calls, worked on a file and dribbled more coffee on his shirt. I sat there looking out the window and thought of one more conversation I had. This one was with Casey out at the airport.

"I am so not kidding. I want that bastard killed, Dev. I don't want him arrested. I don't want him to go to trial. I want him to be dead, Dev, he doesn't deserve to live. Dead. Promise me."

"I'll see what I can do, Casey."

"I'm not fucking around, Dev."

"I gotta take off man, I'm pleading a DUI right after lunch. You gonna be around this afternoon?" Louie asked as he stacked a couple of files into his computer bag. He had two very similar coffee stains on his shirt, one on either side of his tie.

"I'm not sure, I'm working on something and might have to take off."

"Promise me you won't barricade yourself in the office again. Okay?"

"I promise."

He shot a quick glance at the blue bag lying on the floor then said, "You sure you're okay?"

"Yeah, thanks for asking, just thinking through this thing I'm working on."

"Okay, catch you later, wish me luck," he said and closed the door behind him.

I watched him walk out of the building a moment later. He crossed the street to his car then hopped in and headed for downtown.

I set the bag back on my desk. I walked over to the coffeepot and turned it off, then opened the bottom drawer of the file cabinet. Just to play it safe I slipped on a pair of surgical gloves then went back to my desk and printed off a number ten envelope addressed to Tubby Gustafson in care of Jackie Van Dorn. I slipped one of the bands with the penciled '$5000 9/14/11' and the initials into the envelope then taped the envelope closed and stuck a stamp featuring a Purple Heart on the envelope. I kept the gloves on and walked the envelope out to the mailbox across the street.

It was probably overkill, but then again with Tubby Gustafson I wasn't going to take any chances. It would be just like him to have access to a fingerprint data base or some form of DNA testing. I could only hope the currency band would get him thinking back to the half million dollars someone stole from him.

There's an old adage that says something like *'the best place to hide an item is out in the open.'* Yeah maybe, but I didn't think that applied to cold cash. I drove over to the wine store by my house, a place called Solo Vino. Its run by a guy named Chuck. As I walked in the door he looked up from behind the counter.

"I know, you want something with a nice bouquet that will make them lose all self control after just a couple of sips. Oh, and you want it for under five dollars."

"If you had something like that I'd buy a case. Actually, I was wondering if I could grab a box from you. I'm just packing up a couple of things."

"Help yourself," he said and sort of nodded toward the back cooler where a stack of empty boxes stood.

I waved thanks on my way out and Chuck nodded then went back to ringing up someone's purchase. I checked both sides of the street then opened the trunk and stuffed the nylon bag in the wine box. I had to reposition some bundles inside the bag, but after some fooling around it fit. I closed the trunk and drove over to my local bank.

Chapter Thirty-Eight

I rented the largest safety deposit box they had, one-hundred-and-twenty-five bucks for a year. The manager used two small keys to unlock the metal box in the vault. Then she pulled it out and I followed her into a small private cubicle with a door.

"You can just come and get me when you're finished in here and we'll put that back in the vault," she said then glanced at my box touting 'California's Best Wine.'

"Just some old prayer books of my mom's, I keep them for sentimental reasons," I said.

She nodded as if somehow this made perfect sense then closed the door behind her.

I checked the ceiling for cameras and didn't see any. I opened the box, pulled the nylon bag out, unzipped the thing and began stacking bundles of cash in the safety deposit box. I was afraid there wouldn't be enough room, but in the end it all fit. I stuffed the loose bundle of bills I'd removed the band from into my front pocket, and then got the manager to return the box to the vault.

"Wow, a lot of prayer books," she said as she hefted the box back into its space in the vault.

"Yeah, she was very religious, went to church all the time." I smiled.

I felt a lot more relaxed after I left the bank. I drove over to Casey's house and parked in the garage. Two of the contractors were sitting at the kitchen counter looking at a couple of color swatches when I came in.

"Oh, just in time," one of them said. "We're going to be painting on the first floor starting tomorrow. You don't happen to know which colors go where, do you? She told us, but we must have tossed the note," he said then pushed three swatches toward me. One of them was a gray the color of concrete and the other two were similar, but different sort of blues.

It seemed pretty obvious. "This one should be the dining room, this one would look good in the den and then this concrete looking stuff is probably the front room."

"We just put them on the wall and never comment," the other guy said then they both laughed.

I chatted with them for a while. They mentioned they were on schedule and would probably wrap the job up in the next week.

"This is where that guy was killed, right?"

"Yeah, he was a pal of mine, both he and his wife, actually."

"They ever get the guy that shot him?"

"Nope, as far as I know the cops got no idea who it was, or even why for that matter."

"What a shame," one of them said and just shook his head.

"Yeah, everyone loved the guy, just a real nice guy and some jerk does that. It doesn't make any sense," I said.

"There are some folks walking around, that there's really only one way to deal with them. You're not

179

going to rehabilitate them or save their soul. They're the dregs of society."

"Seems to be a lot of that going around," I said.

They nodded and left after a few more minutes. I grabbed a beer and settled in for a quiet night. I was coming out of the shower the next morning and they were already spreading drop cloths getting ready to paint.

As I left, one of them called, "Thanks for your help on where these colors go."

"Glad I could be of service," I said and headed out the door.

Chapter Thirty-Nine

I had just parked in front of my office building when a large black pickup truck came out of nowhere and pulled in directly behind me. Fat Freddy climbed out and walked toward the door of my car. He had on a flowered Hawaiian print shirt, featuring a sky blue background with large red flowers. As he walked, he gobbled one of the half dozen or so cookies he held in his hand. If I had to guess I'd say they were chocolate chip. His nose was still black-and-blue although the swelling looked to be all but gone. I locked the door then lowered the window slightly as he approached.

"Hey, how's it going, man?"

"Fine, Freddy just fine. What can I do for you?"

"I was hoping you might be able to help me out, give me some advice."

"I can give you some advice, but I can't promise it will be any good."

"Maybe hop in my truck and we can talk."

"Your truck? You know I got a call from the police regarding your truck and the little batting lesson you gave your friend Dallas the other night. They wondered if I knew anything. I think they got a report from one of the neighbors."

"What'd you tell them?"

"Its never been very difficult for me to play dumb, Freddy, but maybe next time, promise you'll just leave me completely out of it."

"Come on back and check this ride out, it's really cool."

"Thanks, but no thanks, Freddy. I've got one of those busy days ahead of me and I'd better get cracking."

"Come on back," he said. He gave a quick glance up and down the street then lifted the Hawaiian print shirt and rested his hand on a rather large pistol wedged against his massive stomach.

"You present a persuasive argument." I smiled and climbed out from behind the wheel.

"I knew you'd see things my way, Dev, but just for the sake of pleasant conversation maybe turn around and let me check you, make sure you're not carrying."

"I can tell you, I'm not," I said and smiled my most charming smile.

"Turn around anyway and let's be sure," he said then started to pat me down. His third or fourth pat found the .38 in my front pocket. He pulled it out and looked from me to the gun then back to me.

"Dev, you weren't lying to me, were you?"

"Gee. I guess I just forgot that one."

"Are there any others?"

"No."

"Promise?"

"Yeah, that's it."

"Tell you what, you drive, and I'll ride. That way I can talk and you can listen."

"How could I refuse?"

"Actually, you really can't," Freddy said then he handed me the set of keys he'd torn from Dallas's pocket the other night.

I climbed up into the driver's seat. Freddy stretched out in the passenger seat and faced me with a pistol resting on his lap.

"Where to?" I said as I pulled away from the curb.

"We're gonna watch Bulldog while he makes his collections this morning."

"Bulldog? I'm not so sure that's a good idea, Freddy."

"Oh yeah, and why is that?"

"There was an incident yesterday morning."

"Yesterday morning?"

"Yeah, about four in the morning. Bulldog and two guys I recognized as bouncers at Nasty's paid me a visit. Only it didn't work out like they'd planned," I said then proceeded to fill in some of the details. I didn't mention the money or mailing one of the bands to Tubby Gustafson.

"That dude you shot is one mean hombre," Freddy said.

"Well, he's gonna have some time rolling around in a wheel chair to think about improving his attitude."

"Take a left at the light down here and head over to the East side. That means Bulldog is down to just one guy helping him, Les Hudson, Lester the Molester."

"Never heard of him."

"He's another one of those guys that sucked up to Bulldog, one of the assholes that beat the shit out of me. He had a thing for all the girls at Nasty's and just about all of them wanted nothing to do with him."

"He's that bad?"

Freddy shot me a look. "Didn't you hear? Dude, they call the guy Lester the Molester. The only one who'd have anything to do with him was that old bitch, Cougar, but she was on the weird side anyway, fried when she wasn't just drunk or high."

I nodded, and didn't see any benefit to mentioning the fact I knew her well before she was Cougar.

"Take a left here, down Payne Ave." Freddy said then glanced at the clock on the dash. "Bulldog should be hitting a couple of those fingernail joints right about now. See that Super America up there on the right, about three doors past that just pull in anywhere and we can wait."

I passed the Super America then pulled into the first spot I saw. We were just a few doors away from the nail place. A couple of minutes after I parked two Asian women walked past and entered, I guessed they worked there. About ten minutes after that a long, green Jaguar pulled into a parking place a couple of car lengths ahead of us. The engine remained running as Bulldog stepped out on the passenger side. He briefly glanced up and down the street then walked into the nail place. The moment Bulldog stepped inside Freddy was out of the pickup and waddled quickly toward the Jaguar.

He pulled the gun out of his belt just as he opened the passenger door. The Jaguar tipped heavily to the right as he slid in.

I was thinking about just driving away when he was back out of the Jaguar, it looked like he stopped to pick something up then ran back to the pickup. I had the engine started by the time he opened the door and I was pulling away from the curb just as Bulldog stepped out of the shop and we raced past. Freddy gave a little wave, but I wasn't sure Bulldog saw him then he tossed what looked like a brown paper lunch bag on the seat between us.

"What the hell are you doing, are you crazy? Shit, they'll be right on our ass," I said and checked the side view mirror to see if the Jaguar was after us yet.

"Quit worrying, I slit their tire on the way back, they ain't going anywhere," he said and laughed.

"But they saw you, I mean that Lester guy he knows it's you. He'll tell Bulldog and I'm not sure I really needed this, Freddy. I got enough problems with Bulldog already. I told you they said they were looking for you the other night."

He opened the brown paper bag. It looked like one of the lunch bags I used to take to school as a kid. He pulled out a stack of bills and started counting, after a bit he said, "Eleven hundred bucks, Dev."

"I don't want anything to do with that shit. It's not worth it. Bulldog and Tubby are going to hunt you down, Freddy. That's barely enough for a one way ticket out of town and if I were you I'd be heading out in the next few minutes."

"That's where you're wrong, Dev. I'm not gonna keep this money. I'm gonna turn it over to its rightful owner."

"That's really noble, Freddy, but just a little misguided. Great to give it back to those hardworking folks, but Bulldog will just be back next week for more, and then the week after that. Only next time he won't be so easy to rip off. Oh, and just in case you're not aware, he's gonna come looking for you and he won't be very happy."

"I'm counting on that, Dev. Believe me. As for giving it back to those folks, what the hell are you talking about?"

"You said you were going to turn it over to its rightful owner."

"Yeah, Tubby."

"Tubby?"

"Get this, I have it on pretty good authority Tubby doesn't have a clue about Bulldog's little protection racket. He is gonna freak, man. Take a right here at this next corner."

"Where are we going?"

"Nasty's, Tubby has a lunch meeting with Jackie Van Dorn every Thursday."

__Chapter Forty__

"No offense, but Nasty's is the last place I'm going to," I said then made the right hand turn and checked the mirror just to make sure no one was following.

"Oh, come on, Dev, where's your sense of adventure. No guts, no glory, man."

"I'm on borrowed time as far as taking risks, Freddy and I certainly don't feel the need to cut to my final chapter by getting involved with Jackie Van Dorn, or worse Tubby Gustafson.

"Dev, I'm bringing over eleven hundred bucks to Tubby as proof Bulldog is ripping him off. What's the problem?"

"The problem is you can't trust any of them. Tubby's liable to take the money and turn you over to Bulldog just for something to watch. You can't get on his good side, because the man doesn't have one."

"Okay, suit yourself. I'm giving you the perfect opportunity to get in on the glory, but if you don't want any, who am I to tell you that you're an absolute dumb shit."

"Just leave me out of it."

"Consider it done, Dev. Oh, turn in here and you can drop me off at the dumpsters in back."

"God, I don't want to even be here."

"Will you relax, what can happen?"

I pulled into Nasty's parking lot then drove around the building to the back and dropped Freddy off next to the dumpster's. They didn't smell any better than the last time I was back here. I watched him press the buzzer then look up into the security camera and talk, although I couldn't hear what was being said. A moment later he opened the door and stepped inside. That was good enough for me and I started to back out just as some sort of car painted flat black backed into the lane and parked there, effectively blocking me in.

I gave a couple of polite beeps on the horn, suggesting the guy take his head out of his ass. That got him to step out of his car, come around to the side of his car closest to me then just lean back against the car door, fold his arms and look bored.

I beeped again and he just shook his head and remained looking awfully bored.

I was effectively trapped. I climbed out of the truck and walked toward the guy. He nodded at me as I approached.

"You got me blocked in and I was just leaving."

"Not really," he said. "Yeah, I got you blocked in, but apparently they'd like you to hang around for a few minutes. Might as well climb back into your truck and just wait. How you liking that ride anyway? I think Dallas has one just like that."

"He didn't seem to be kidding and I sure as hell wasn't going to tell him. It's okay, nice ride, bit of a gas-hog though."

He nodded then sort of looked bored and gazed across the parking lot toward the street. I climbed back in the truck. Fat Freddy came out about fifteen minutes later. As he climbed in the cab I noticed a reddish ring covering his upper lip, a wine stain.

"Everything okay?" I asked.

"Piece of cake, man. You should have come with."

"I had my own meeting," I said and jerked a thumb out the back window to where the flat black car had been parked just a moment ago. Fat Freddy turned and looked out the back window then looked at me like I was nuts.

"There was some guy back there blocking me in. Said he got word I was supposed to wait, I don't know where he went."

"Well, he's not blocking you now so let's get going."

I backed out from the dumpsters, then made my way out of Nasty's lot as quickly as possible. "Did you get to see him, Tubby?"

"Yeah, nice guy. I'd seen him before, but never got to really talk to the man. He was nice, thanked me for the nine-hundred bucks and said he'd have a little talk with Bulldog."

"Wait a minute, nine hundred bucks? I thought you counted out over eleven hundred thirty minutes ago."

"Dev, it's how the big guys do it. Everyone takes a percentage. Let me tell you something, you know what those guys were doing before I went up to Van Dorn's office? I'll tell you, they were counting cash. They hid the stuff before I came in, but I saw the band that had wrapped it up, five grand worth. Can you believe it? Five grand they're counting out over lunch, that's how the big guys do it, Dev. What? You never watched the Soprano's?"

"This isn't some stupid ass TV show, Freddy. God, five grand? Was it a paper band and five grand was written in pencil with a date and maybe some initials?"

"How'd you know that?"

"I don't believe it. And you think Tubby's going to talk to Bulldog? Well, you're probably right. That's just perfect. I don't see any problem there except that Bulldog will know you and probably me as well, were involved in your stupid little robbery. After he gets done denying everything he's going to come after the both of us."

"Oh yeah, well he's not going to find me. I'll be like a ghost, man. Yeah, you know maybe that's it, a new sort of persona, my new brand. They'll call me The Phantom or Mr. Mysterious, get it?"

"No, Freddy, I don't get it. I do know you just paid Tubby nine hundred bucks. Bulldog will deny everything and convince Tubby you're the liar. What about me, Freddy? You think I want that psychotic nut job Bulldog looking for me, where the hell am I going to go?"

"Why would he be looking for you?"

"Because you made me drive you around, Freddy. He'll think we're partners. He'll think I was in on the whole thing."

"Can't you just explain it to him? Tell him it wasn't your idea."

"Yeah, that'll work, gee, now why didn't I think of that? Explain it to Bulldog? He's nuts, Freddy, a whacko, I keep telling you. You said it yourself, he's the one who assaulted you, did that to your face, took black beauty and after he smashed it up trying to kill Casey, he set it on fire."

"Oh, yeah," Freddy said suddenly sounding deep in thought. You could see the wheels slowly beginning to turn in his mind. "Think this could be a problem?"

I drove back to my office, climbed out of the truck and Freddy took off. We hadn't come up with any sort of plan. I quickly came to the conclusion things would work out a lot better for me if I could just get some distance between me and Freddy. I spent the afternoon at the window, looking up and down the street when I wasn't watching the front door to the building. Bulldog never showed up.

Chapter Forty-One

I spent the next three days looking over my shoulder and sleeping behind the couch in Casey's front room. I expected Bulldog to arrive at any moment. I hadn't heard a word from Fat Freddy, and Casey had phoned the last two days wondering when she could come home.

I was convinced it was just a matter of time before Bulldog made a play, but time seemed to be dragging. About the only positive thing that had happened was the contractors had finished, packed up all their tools and were gone.

Now Casey's home was too nice for the likes of me. The rooms were freshly painted, the light fixtures were wired and actually working, the kitchen cabinet doors were hung, granite countertops had replaced the sheets of plywood painted black and the bathroom fixtures were all new and sparkling.

After two more days and four phone calls from Casey, I was starting to dial down. Maybe Bulldog had turned his attention into finding Fat Freddy and those two could just work out whatever the final solution would be.

My phone rang late in the afternoon.

"Haskell Investigations."

"Dev, Casey."

I'd already spoken to her twice today. This wasn't going to be good.

"Promise me you won't get mad?"

"I don't know what you're going to tell me, Casey. So, how can I promise if I don't know?"

"I want to come home."

"We've had this conversation before, I think the last one was about ninety minutes ago."

"Don't get mad, I don't need that right now."

"I'm not mad, yet."

"I'm going crazy down here, it's been fun and everything, but I need to come home. I'm tired of running, Dev."

"Running? What do you mean running? From what I can tell you've been having a blast, which is more than I can say for some of us up here."

"I'm going stir crazy."

"And you're safe."

"I don't care about that, Dev."

"I do, just hold on for a little longer. If it's about money, don't worry I can send you some. How much do you need?"

"It's not about money, Dev. Right now it's about my sanity. I need to get back up there."

"No, Casey."

"I already booked a flight."

"What?"

"You heard me, I booked a flight. I'll be back up there two days from now. I'll call you from the airport for a ride, Dev?"

"Casey, if you come back up here, I don't know that I can protect you. The guy I think murdered

Dermot is still out there. I've no idea where he is or what his plans are. I only know it can't be good."

"I don't care," she said and meant it.

"And I can't talk you out of this?"

"No, you can't."

"It's a bad idea, Casey."

"We'll see," she said and hung up.

I went down to The Spot, it had been close to a week since I'd darkened the door. I spent the entire night telling lies and buying most of the rounds. I closed the place and took the back streets home. I pulled into the garage then walked through the backyard to the deck. I was halfway up the steps when I saw the back door. It was partially open and from the looks of the frame, the door had been kicked in. Splinters and bits of the frame lay on the floor of the back room and the area around the lock on the door looked cracked. Whoever did this must have had a pretty heavy boot.

I went back to the garage and got a pistol out of the glove compartment then cautiously returned to the house. I carefully stepped into the back room, quietly pushed the damaged door closed then listened for any telltale noise.

I couldn't hear anything, but just to play it safe I slipped off my shoes before I quietly started going through, searching the entire first floor room by room in the dark. I didn't want to turn on a light for fear it would alert any intruder still here.

The odds of some random knucklehead deciding to kick in the door were slim to nonexistent. There was only one name rattling around in my brain, Bulldog. I cautiously crept up the stairs to the second floor then started the process all over again, searching the place room by room in the dark.

194

The pounding of my heart was getting louder as I worked my way down the hall. The door to the back bedroom was closed. I waited in the hall for a good five minutes, positive Bulldog was in there and just waiting for me.

I finally pushed the door only to find it was closed, firmly. I crouched down and slowly turned the knob, after a long moment the knob clicked and I leapt forward into the room rolling on the floor with my pistol up ready to fire. The adrenaline was rushing through my veins and my entire system was on high alert. Thankfully, the room was empty.

I approached the closet where the cabinet with the secret panel was, the absolute last place in the house to search.

"I'll give you till the count of five to come out or I'm going to shoot," I said.

I counted slowly, "One, two." At three I went in, finger on the trigger ready to fire. The room was empty, I was breathing heavily, sweating and now stone cold sober. I turned on the light.

The drawers were haphazardly thrown off to the side and the panel at the back of the cabinet was wide open. I was willing to bet whoever was here, and my educated guess was Bulldog, was probably in the house for no more than two minutes. He most likely stormed up here, tossed the drawers to the side and then got the disappointment of his life.

I closed the panel, set the drawers back in the cabinet then turned on the lights as I walked back downstairs. I carried an upholstered chair from the front room through the kitchen and wedged it against the back door, then placed a couple of beer bottles against the door so if someone did happen to come back during the night they'd tip over the bottles and hopefully alert me.

I went through the first floor, this time with the lights on. As near as I could determine nothing had been damaged. As I settled in to sleep on the floor behind the couch in the front room I was positive it had been Bulldog, the nagging concern was, now what?

I think I slept for maybe a total of twenty minutes the rest of the night, and not all at once. What was Bulldog's next move? Would he think the money was stolen by one of the renters while he was serving time? Would he blame Dermot and Casey? The only thing I was sure about was that Bulldog was not the sort of psychopath to just give up.

My thoughts became more positive with the sunrise. I called the contractor first thing that morning and explained the break-in damage to the back door. They were there by midmorning making the necessary repairs. By noon I'd calmed down substantially, although it was a fairly warm day I was wearing a sport coat over my T-shirt to cover the shoulder holster.

The rest of the day was mercifully uneventful and I was back at Casey's place before dinner. As calm as I thought I was, I did do another search of the house with my pistol drawn ready to shoot. The only thing I found out of order was a coffee mug one of the contractors had left in the back room.

Chapter Forty-Two

My phone rang about a half hour later. I had my shoes off, feet up on the coffee table, and I was beginning to relax.

"Haskell Investigations."

"Dev, are you busy?" It was Heidi and she sounded frantic.

"You okay?"

"God, I saw a mouse in the kitchen."

"You should probably go get some traps at the hardware store."

"Traps? Can't you come over here and get him."

"Oh, God. Maybe he'll just go away."

"Dev!"

"Okay, okay, just relax."

"Relax? Are you kidding? You know what they say if you see one you've got a hundred or something."

"I don't think you have a hundred. What could they live on? You never cook."

"Could you please just come over, please, please? I promise I will be very grateful." she said.

That last part sounded pretty good. "I'll be there in about twenty minutes."

"Don't take any longer, the thing could be breeding right now. And bring your gun, maybe two guns."

I took my time. I showered, shaved, brushed my teeth, put on some clean clothes and picked up a bottle of wine at Solo Vino. Then I went to the hardware store and got some traps and poison. When I pulled up in front of her house, Heidi was sitting out on her front steps. She almost ran to the car.

"What took you so long?"

"I'm sorry, I was in the middle of something when you called."

"Probably a beer."

"You want this taken care of? Or, are you just going to bitch me out?"

"God, I'm afraid to go back into my own house. He ran right along the kitchen wall, the little bastard."

"The thing is about this big," I made a two inch gap between my thumb and forefinger.

"Just get him out of there."

"Here, I brought you a bottle of wine," I said and handed her the bottle.

"Believe me this isn't enough," she said. "What's in the bag?"

"Some traps and poison and…"

"I don't want you to catch him, I want the thing killed and out of my house, isn't that what you do for a living?"

"No, not exactly. I tell you what, why don't you go pick up some dinner, here's some cash," I said and pulled out two twenties from my front pocket. "I'll deal with this."

"Okay, my car keys are on the kitchen counter, I think."

I gave her a look.

"I'm not going back in there, Dev."

"All right, let me get them for you, princess."

I got her car keys and handed them to her out in the front yard. "Did you see him?"

"Yeah, he told me his name was Mickey."

"This isn't funny, Dev," she said and hit me on the shoulder, then suddenly she looked like she was on the verge of crying.

"I'll deal with it, Heidi. You go pick up some dinner and take your time."

She nodded and half ran to her car. I retreated to her kitchen. As usual there was virtually no food in the house except for some crackers and rice cakes in a cupboard above the stove. Everything else was in a can. There were two take out Styrofoam containers in the refrigerator which I didn't have the courage to open and a bottle of mineral water. I found a jar of peanut butter in another cupboard. I baited the traps with peanut butter and some of the puffed rice cake. I figured he'd either get caught in the trap or once he saw what there was food-wise he would just take off and go to another house.

Heidi returned a good hour later. She rang the doorbell.

"Oh it's you," I said when I opened the door.

"Did you get him?" she whined.

"Yes," I lied.

She opened the door, gave me a big kiss and suddenly seemed her old sexy self. "I got a bunch of take out and some more wine," she said and walked into the kitchen.

I followed.

"Did you shoot him?"

"No, I set one of the traps and he just threw himself onto it, sort of a suicide thing I guess."

"You did get him, right?"

"Yes, he's out in your trash bin. I set some traps under your sink just in case there might be another one, but I didn't see any signs."

"Oh, God, I hope not. I don't know if I could deal with another one."

"Hopefully you won't have to, what's for dinner?"

"There's this great little Thai place I just love so we can eat healthy and it will taste good, too."

I must have made a face at the word healthy.

"I think you can miss out on pizza just one night and you'll live."

Chapter Forty-Three

We were working our way through the second bottle of wine, Heidi was laughing, feeling no pain and completely relaxed. I wasn't far behind her and after the past couple of days it was feeling pretty good.

It was one of those pregnant pause moments. We'd been joking and laughing and then we were suddenly quiet for the briefest of seconds at exactly the same time. The unmistakable sound of a mouse trap snapping reverberated through the kitchen like a howitzer going off. Then we heard high pitched squeaking coming from under the kitchen sink.

Heidi looked at me, whined, "Dev" and jumped off her kitchen stool and onto the kitchen counter, kicking over the wine bottle in the process. "Dev, do something, damn it."

The squeaking continued and occasionally something rattled from under the sink. My first thought was to just shoot through the cabinet door.

"God, Dev, don't just stand there stupid, do something. I think he's trying to open the door."

"I was going to clean up the wine you spilled."

"Leave that. Oh my God, listen to that thing. Do you think he's hurt?" she said and then her eyes began to tear up.

I didn't want to open up the cabinet door, but I was running out of options when all of a sudden the squeaking stopped.

"Oh, God, now what?" Heidi half screamed, she was still on top of the kitchen counter with her legs drawn up and her arms wrapped around them. Her face was buried between her knees.

"I think I better open another bottle of wine."

"Don't you dare, not until you deal with that," she said and pointed beneath her kitchen sink.

"All right, all right," I said then took a deep breath and cautiously opened the cabinet expecting to see a dead mouse. Instead the thing jumped onto the kitchen floor dragging the trap behind him.

Heidi shrieked.

The thing startled me and I went to stomp him with my foot. It must have been the wine because I missed and just caught the trap. The pressure was enough to cut his tail off and the little bastard shot across the kitchen floor, minus his tail and dripping blood along the way.

"Oh my God," Heidi screamed.

He was at the kitchen door trying desperately to squeeze underneath and getting stopped by the riser on the floor.

Heidi continued screeching.

I grabbed the wine bottle off the floor and backhanded it at him. The bottle caught him just as he rose up on his hind legs. He splattered in a bloody mess against her white enamel kitchen door.

"Oh, God, I can't look, I can't look. Clean it up, Dev. Get rid of it, please. I'll do anything, just get it out of my house."

I grabbed a handful of paper towels and wiped up what was left of the mouse, then picked up the trap and opened the drawer with the wastebasket. I dropped everything in the wastebasket then pulled the trash bag out, knotted it and marched out to her trash bin.

Heidi was still on the kitchen counter when I came back in. I wet some more paper towels, cleaned up the little trail of blood running across her kitchen tiles then wiped the door clean. I sprayed some Windex on the door for added measure and wiped that off.

"I'll be back in a moment, I expect you to be off the counter and sitting on the kitchen stool by the time I return."

She stuck her tongue out at me, but didn't say anything.

By the time I came back in the kitchen, she was on the stool, but she was sitting cross legged making sure her feet were nowhere near the floor.

"How would it be if I opened another bottle of wine and we can put this all behind us? Maybe you'd feel more comfortable in your living room." I said. I was on my hands and knees, mopping up wine from the kitchen floor with a sponge.

"I'll wait for you out there," she said and quickly exited the room. She was back to happy a glass of wine later.

We both slept in late the next morning, but only because we were up a good portion of the night paying and collecting the debt. Just in case any little visitors might still be lingering, I banged around the kitchen while I put the coffee on the next morning, then I went out and picked up caramel rolls and we enjoyed a leisurely breakfast.

Chapter Forty-Four

I didn't make it into the office until well past the noon hour. I'd gone home to get cleaned up then swung by Casey's just to check on things. Everything looked fine, both the front and back door were in one piece. I was still worried about her coming back to town tomorrow, but there was absolutely nothing I could do about it. I could only hope Bulldog assumed one of the low-life renters he'd brought in had gotten their hands on the money and disappeared.

I thought it might not be a bad idea to check in on Swindle Lawless, aka Cougar to see if Bulldog had tried to shake her down. If she was the main attraction at Nasty's for the after-work-banker crowd I figured she probably arrived an hour before, right around four. I was in the parking lot waiting for her.

She drove in about fifteen minutes before she was due to go on stage. I might have missed her, in fact I was ready to take off after sitting in the parking lot for the better part of an hour waiting for her to show up. At first I thought it was a motorcycle with rumbling pipes, then I saw the Lincoln with the cracked windshield, buckled hood and the trunk held down with an elastic cord.

Swindle pulled into a parking place, scraping the side of someone's car in the process. An alarm sounded on the car and she backed out of the spot then hurriedly pulled into another spot a row over. I was pretty sure she'd been talking to Bulldog. At least I thought it was probably a safe guess once I saw her black eye.

"Swindle," I called and then hurried to cut her off before she made it to the 'Employee's Only' door. The car alarm continued to chirp.

She attempted to dodge me and go around the far side of another car, but I was too fast and caught up to her.

"Hold on, Swindle, I just wanted to talk to you for a moment."

"Not really interested, sweetheart," she said then looked at me and said, "Hey, I know you, don't I? How'd you know my name?"

"Yeah, Swindle, it's me, Dev Haskell. I was buying you some shots the other night, hoping to get a little more personal, but it didn't quite work out."

"There's always tonight, Denny."

"What's with the eye?" I asked.

"Oh nothing, a little misunderstanding is all, someone thinking wrong, or just not thinking at all."

"Your friend Bulldog?"

"That son-of-a-bitch better watch it if he knows what's good for him. Accusing me of stealing. I got no idea what in the hell he's even talking about."

"I heard he's been shaking down a lot of folks."

"Not you, too. Why is everyone suddenly interested in Bulldog? First it was Tubby, then that young fool that was the bouncer."

"Fat Freddy?"

"That's the one. Why all the sudden interest in Bulldog? Ungrateful is what he is, he ain't getting' anymore from me after the other night, that's for damn sure. He's cut off as far as I'm concerned. Not that he was any good at gettin' it up, anyway. Look, we should maybe link up after, I'll give you a discount, but I'm on in a couple of minutes. All them suits just can't seem to get enough of old Cougar. What'd you say your name was again?"

"Dev."

"I'll remember that and I'll be looking for you in there, Des. You just remember to tip me real nice now, hear."

"Yeah, Swindle, I'll do that."

She headed toward the 'Employee's Only' door, unbuttoning her blouse along the way. She punched in a code on the key pad and by the time she had the door open the blouse was hanging over her arm. She'd just begun to undo her belt when the door closed behind her.

As I walked back to my car I thought, 'Well, there was my answer, Bulldog was still looking.' The car she scraped was chirping intermittently now. I couldn't think of anywhere else to go so I headed down to The Spot.

Chapter Forty-Five

I hadn't been at the bar for very long and for all practical purposes I'd been behaving myself. Mike was bartending and I was content to sip and just think. Casey was due back in town tomorrow and after seeing Swindle sporting a black eye I had fresh concerns. I had just signaled Mike for another when my phone rang.

"Haskell Investigations."

"Dev?"

It was Heidi and she sounded frightened. I really didn't feel like dealing with another mouse. "Yeah, Heidi, what's up?"

A rough voice snarled across the phone, "You better get you ass over here if you ever want to enjoy your little friend, again."

The juke box was playing. People were talking and laughing. Mike was sliding a fresh pint across the bar to me. I was unaware of everything except Bulldog on the other end of the phone.

"I'm coming, so help me, you touch her and I'll kill you."

"Sure you will," Bulldog laughed. "Better hurry or we're gonna start without you," he said then hung up.

I left Mike holding the beer with a shocked look on his face and ran to my car. I pulled a U-turn across Randolph and blasted through the red light on the corner. I was climbing the hill, doing about sixty on the city street and picking up speed. At the Lexington stoplight I veered into the right turn only lane, gave a quick look then shot through another red light. I figured Bulldog heard me from a block away as I skidded around the corner then screeched to a stop halfway up the block in front of Heidi's house. There was a long green Jaguar parked across the street. I was pretty sure it was the same vehicle Fat Freddy slit the tire on the other day after he stole Bulldog's protection money.

I hurried out of my car and ran across the front lawn pulling the pistol out of my belt as I went. The front door was wide open and all the lights in the house were off. I jumped up the front steps, stepped inside the house and waited. My heart was pounding so loudly I couldn't hear anything else. My eyes began to grow accustomed to the dark and I could begin to make out the shapes of living room furniture.

"Maybe just set the piece on that table against the wall," a voice growled from a far corner. I could just barely make out two figures, it looked like Bulldog had Heidi on his lap.

"Are you okay, Heidi?"

"Just do like I said or the bitch is going to get it."

"Let her go, Bulldog. She can't help you with whatever it is you want."

"This is the last time I'm telling you, dumb shit. Put that gun down or your girlfriend is going to have a great big hole in her pretty little head."

"It's down, Bulldog, I'm putting it down," I said and set the pistol on the small table then I turned to face Bulldog and raised my hands.

"Move away from that table," he said.

"Are you okay, Heidi?"

"She might be coming with me, Haskell. I kind of like the way we seem to fit together," he laughed then bounced her on his lap and grabbed her chest.

A slight sound seemed to escape from her lips.

"I'm looking for something I lost, Haskell. Your name keeps coming up."

"If you mean that protection money, I heard that was Fat Freddy. I didn't have anything to do with that."

"Except drive the truck, I seen ya, you were there helping him. You think I'm stupid? We'll get to that money later. Right now, I think you know what the hell I'm talking about."

"I don't have a clue what you're talking about."

"Oh really, maybe this'll refresh your memory," he said then hit Heidi across the back of her head. She fell off his lap with a groan, he quickly reached down and pulled her head up by the hair and then held on.

"I'm really running out of patience here, Haskell. I could use a little cooperation from you right about now," he said then yanked Heidi by her hair again.

"I already told you, I got no idea what in the hell you're talking about."

"Oh, really? Funny, ain't it? Everyone I talked to so far said pretty much the same thing. The difference was they were so scared to death they were shitting themselves. You on the other hand, I got a feeling you know. You're just such a stupid son-of-a-bitch you think you can play me."

"If I knew what you wanted I'd give it to you, honest. But I don't know, I don't." I made my voice sound pleading hoping he'd buy it.

"Bullshit, you know what I'm talking about, it was in a nylon bag. And I'm through playing games with you. You think you're so fucking smart? Someone tried to be cute and sent Tubby a currency band in the mail. So I asked myself, now, who in the hell would know to send that to Tubby? Most of the folks I talked to can't see much past their next drink or score. They only read about Tubby in the papers, they've never seen him, wouldn't know a hell of a lot about him and certainly wouldn't know that Jackie Van Dorn was his attorney. What sort of asshole do you think would know that sort of thing?"

"I was talking to Van Dorn about a real estate matter. That's all. Its common knowledge the only client he has is Tubby. Hell, I got that information from the cops."

"A real estate matter. Hear that, baby doll?" he said then yanked Heidi's hair again and she gave a sort of yelp.

"Just let her go, I'll do anything you want."

"You know what I want, Haskell, that bag, get it."

"Let her go, Bulldog I don't know anything about a bag."

"When I get what's mine, then you get her back. Until then, we're just gonna sit back and party, aren't we, baby?" he said then ran a pistol along the side of Heidi's face and kissed her on the top of the head.

Heidi let out a small groan.

"You got till noon tomorrow then all bets are off. You can just contact me on your little fuck-buddies phone. You or anyone else shows up here unannounced and you can kiss her nice firm ass goodbye. Now get out of here before I change my mind."

"Bulldog, I don't…"

"You heard me, get the hell out of here," he shouted.

I turned to go then slowly began to reach for the pistol I placed on the table.

"Leave it and get out of here now or so help me."

"Just go, Dev, and do whatever he wants, please." Heidi cried.

"You heard the lady, dumbass, get moving."

Chapter Forty-Six

I walked out to my car and drove off. I parked two
blocks away then ran back down the alley to Heidi's.
There was a light on in one of the guest rooms on the
second floor, but other than that the house was dark. I
crept through the neighbor's garden to the front of the
house, the door had been closed.

Even if I had a key I wouldn't be able to get in and
surprise him, and then there was the matter of Heidi's
safety. I planned to be at the bank in the morning as
soon as they opened up.

I was pretty sure I was safe from Bulldog for the
rest of the night so I attempted to sleep at Casey's.
Attempted is the operative word, I didn't sleep a wink.
At just before sunrise I went down to the office and
pulled the .38 and the blue nylon bag out of my desk
drawer. Then I set about cutting reams of paper into the
size of twenty dollar bills. I placed a twenty on the top
and bottom of each stack and ran a length of blue
masking tape Casey's contractor had left behind around
each bundle. When it was finished it looked sort of
convincing, maybe, if you didn't look too closely. I
took the remaining bundle of twenties from my pocket
and ran a length of tape around it then hauled

everything including the corrugated wine box out to my car.

I phoned Bulldog on Heidi's phone about 9:30.

"Haskell?" he answered.

"Let me speak to Heidi, I want to make sure she's all right."

"She's fine, can't wipe the smile off her face after all the fun we had last night. Didn't we have a good time, sweetheart? Too bad you couldn't join us, Haskell," he laughed.

"Let me talk to her or you won't see a cent of this money."

That seemed to get his attention, because suddenly she was on the line. "Dev?"

"Are you okay, Heidi?"

"Yeah," she said, but she sounded like she was ready to burst into tears.

"There, happy, asshole?" Bulldog said.

"Here's what we're going to do, Bulldog. I want you…"

"I'm the one telling you how this is gonna go down, you piece of shit."

"No, I don't think so, I'm the guy with your money. When I pull up I want you to let her go. She can get in her car and drive away. I'll stay in her place."

"I said…"

"And I said all you're interested in is your money. So shut up and you'll get it. I just want her out of there. I'll call you when I'm out in front," I said and hung up. Then I waited for two very long minutes staring at my phone to see if it would ring. It didn't.

I pulled in behind Bulldog's Jaguar fifteen minutes later. I got out, opened the back door, took out the blue nylon bag and placed it on the roof of my car. I walked around the side of the house to Heidi's back door and called her phone.

"I seen ya pull up, what the hell are you doing in back?"

"I told you before, I want you to let her go."

"Get your ass to the front and we'll talk about it."

"No, I want her at the back door, she can leave and you got me to beat up or kill or whatever makes you happy. But just let her go or you get nothing. I'm only going to wait one minute. Then I'm leaving."

"I'll blow your God damn brains out," he screamed into the phone.

"Go ahead, but then you may not get your money, fifty-fifty shot, Bulldog, after waiting all this time are you willing to gamble?" I said then hung up.

I heard the front door open and thought 'Oh no, he didn't go for it.' But then, just as he was coming down the steps a vehicle pulled in front of the house across the street and Bulldog quickly walked around the side toward me. He was grasping Heidi firmly by the arm and holding a pistol against her rib cage. She had a wild look on her face.

"Just let her go, Bulldog. Just let her walk out the back gate."

"You go get that bag and bring it up here, then we'll see."

"Nope. I've learned the hard way I can't trust you. I got something for you, though. Just to show you I'm on the level. It's in my front pocket, I'm gonna take it out so don't shoot me."

"What the hell is it?"

"Can I get in my pocket? Just watch, I promise no tricks," I said then reached in carefully and slowly pulled out the bundle of twenties with the blue masking tape around it.

At first he just stared, but then his eyes brightened as I held the bundle of cash out toward him.

"Just to show you it's all for real, Bulldog. Now, just let her go. This is the bundle I took the band off of and sent it to Tubby. The rest of the cash is in that bag, so just let her go."

Bulldog looked at me and attempted to smile then snatched the cash out of my hand and stuffed it in his pocket. He grabbed onto Heidi again before either one of us realized what he'd done. "I gotta say, you really are one stupid, dumb son-of-a-bitch. Now I got the both of you and I got the gun. You so much as blink and she get's it first."

"But, I thought we had a deal."

"Shut the fuck up and lets go down and see what's in that bag. You first, dumb shit." Then he motioned with his pistol toward my car. I was trying to come up with an escape plan and failing miserably. Heidi shot a look at me that was a combination of fear and the promise she would kill me as soon as she got the chance.

For the first time, I noticed the vehicle parked across the street was a shiny black pickup with chrome letters just behind the front wheel that said F-350, 4x4. It had dual rear wheels and very large mud flaps.

"That's far enough," Bulldog said as I crossed the sidewalk. We were all standing on the boulevard, gathered around my car like we were just saying a friendly little goodbye. "Get that thing off the roof of your car and open it up," he said then half motioned with his pistol again, not that I needed a reminder.

I pulled the bag off the roof of the car and unzipped it. If he looked closely at the bundles he was liable to shoot the both of us. I dropped the bag on the boulevard and took half a step back.

"Oh, my God," Heidi said.

Bulldog motioned with the pistol for me to step back further, he chuckled as he stared down at the bag and growled, "It's about God damn time." Then he reached down to fan one of the bundles and I knew we were screwed.

"Wait a minute what the hell is…"

But he never finished, the rear door flew open, catching Bulldog across the top of his skull with a dull thunk and sending him backwards onto the sidewalk, unconscious.

Fat Freddy pried himself out of my back seat holding a pistol. "Woo-hoo-hoo. You guys see that? I got him. How's it feel, Bulldog? Happy?" he said then kicked Bulldog on the chin and shoved the pistol into his belt. "God, does that ever feel good."

"Freddy where in the hell did you come from?"

"You kidding? I been following you for almost three days. I thought she was maybe Bulldog's main squeeze or something, but I guess I was wrong on that."

Heidi looked ready to kill.

Bulldog started to move his head back and forth and Freddy handed me a pistol then ran across the street to the truck. He came back with a pair of handcuffs and quickly rolled Bulldog half over and cuffed his hands behind his back. Bulldog growled as he began to regain consciousness.

"Maybe you could help me get him in the back of the truck here would you, Dev?"

"Will he stay back there, is it safe?" I asked as we hoisted Bulldog up onto his feet and began to walk him across the street. He was still groggy from the blow to his head and he staggered.

Freddy lowered the rear gate on the truck and we threw Bulldog up onto the bed like so much dead weight. Then Freddy climbed up, grabbed Bulldog by the collar and dragged him toward the front of the truck. He took a chain attached to the back of cab and wrapped it around Bulldog's neck three or four times. "There, that should hold him," he said.

"Will he be able to breathe?"

"Really not my problem, pal. You mind following me, just in case?"

"Yeah, I guess I can do that." I glanced across the street at Heidi who looked like she was about to have steam come out of her ears. I figured maybe some distance until she cooled down wouldn't be too bad an idea.

Freddy waddled back across the street and grabbed the blue nylon bag. "Sorry, Dev, but finder's keepers," he said then touched the pistol crammed into his belt suggesting *'Don't even think of trying anything.'*

"Are you a policeman?" Heidi asked.

"Yeah, can't you tell by the handcuffs? We're going to take him down to the station, now, aren't we, Haskell," Freddy said.

"Give me half a minute here, Freddy." I said hoping to diffuse the potential eruption from Heidi.

"Are you okay, Heidi?"

"You complete and utter bastard. You got me mixed up in this, this insane situation. Thank God that cop had enough sense to know sooner or later you'd have things all screwed up. Just get the hell out of my sight and don't you ever, never, ever contact me again. Do you hear me?" she screamed as I backed up and quickly made my way into my car. I locked the doors sensing Heidi might want to be left alone, which, being a caring sensitive guy I understood.

Chapter Forty-Seven

I followed behind Freddy, fortunately Bulldog had slumped down on the bed of the truck and couldn't be seen. Freddy took a round about way along the river bluff, then ambled across the 35E Bridge. He exited on the far end of the bridge then drove down along the river on the Lilydale road. He took his sweet time and it was pretty obvious we weren't going anywhere near the police station.

This was relatively unused parkland without so another vehicle on the road. All the activity was on the other side of the river. Freddy pulled off on a small seldom-used gravel road that was more weeds than anything else, then stopped maybe twenty yards in. We were hidden from the road we'd just left by large cottonwood trees and shoulder high growth. The river bank was thick with weeds and I could hear the river, but couldn't see it. Just off to the side was a scorched patch of weeds and low hanging branches, bits of melted plastic and what looked like shattered car window glistened in the sun.

"What are we stopping here for?" I asked.

"Don't you recognize it? This is where that bastard torched black beauty?" Freddy said.

"I thought you were going to bring him to the police?"

"You gotta be kidding me, you can't tell me you really believed that shit, did you?"

"Well no, of course not, but what are you going to do with him?"

"We'll see," Freddy said and lowered the gate on the pick up. Bulldog was lying on the bed of the truck with the chain wrapped tightly around his neck and not looking too good. His face was close to navy-blue and his tongue looked thick and was hanging out of his mouth. His eyes were open and gave off a glassy stare. He wasn't moving.

"Jesus Christ, he's choking," I yelled.

"With any luck the son-of-a-bitch is dead. He stopped kicking about a mile or two after we left. I figured taking my time along the scenic route would probably do the trick."

"What are you going to do with him?"

"Well, we can't dump him in the river, I mean that would be pollution, you know." Freddy settled onto the gate of the pickup then groaned as he stood and stepped back toward the cab. He knelt alongside Bulldog and looked down at him.

"God, he was a real bastard, the list is long of folks who'd like to see this," he said then unwrapped the chain from around Bulldog's neck and let his head drop onto the bed of the pickup with a hollow thunk. He took his time wrapping the chain up on a hook attached to the back of the cab, acting like he had just finished hauling a piece of furniture. Then he grabbed Bulldog's body by the feet and dragged it onto the gate of the truck. The truck bounced a couple of times as Freddy jumped down and I felt the ground around me sort of shudder when he landed.

"Are you gonna just leave him here?"

"You got a better idea?" he said then pulled a pistol from his belt, ejected the clip and the round in the chamber.

"Hand me that bullet there, will you, Dev. I don't feel like bending down. I'll tell you, this is work. But still, safety first," he said then shoved the empty pistol into Bulldog's belt.

"What are you doing?"

"You can thank me later. Oh, almost forgot," he said then grabbed the bundle of cash from Bulldogs pocket. "Don't even ask, man."

"Not to worry, Freddy, you certainly earned it."

Chapter Forty-Eight

Casey phoned from the airport around mid-afternoon. I'd sort of been sitting at my desk in a trance.

"Haskell Investigations."

"Hi, Dev, will you come and pick me up?"

"Yeah, I can be there in about fifteen minutes."

"You're not still mad, are you?"

"No, I'm not mad, Casey."

She was waiting at door number four on the lower level. It was pretty busy and there were a lot of double-parked cars picking folks up. I saw Casey standing on the curb scanning the cars looking for me. I honked and flashed my lights. She ran toward me, opened the back door and threw her suitcase in. Then she climbed in the front seat and looked at me sheepishly.

"Promise you're not still mad?"

"I told you on the phone, no, I'm not mad, Casey. Of course, no one else listens to me, so I don't know why you would." But I meant it as a joke and smiled when I said it which seemed to let some pressure off.

On the short drive to her home we made idle chit-chat. She told me about New Orleans, the things she'd seen, some of the things she'd done. I pulled in front of her place, got her suit case out of the back seat and followed her up to the front porch.

"Oh it's so good to be back here. I just needed to get back, Dev. I need to be in the house. I don't know, now I just wish I could stay here. I mean it was ours, our plan, our dream. God," she said and then just sort of trailed off.

"Come on in and see the work they've done, it looks great," I said then unlocked the front door and stepped back so she could go in.

She took four steps in past the door and said, "Are you kidding me?" Then she just stood staring at the front room.

"Gorgeous isn't it?"

"No, it's painted the wrong color. How could they screw that up? Oh, God, look at the dining room," she said walking toward the back of the house. Then she stepped across the hallway and opened the door. "And the den, too. They painted them all the wrong colors. What were they thinking? How could they get it all mixed up like that?"

"Wow, I have no idea what they were thinking."

"Well, it's still nice to be here. I just wish there was a way for me to stay. Dermot would just love to see everything finished."

"I think he knows, Casey. Hey look, hang on for a minute. I gotta get something out of the car." I ran out to the car, then came back in. "Casey?" I called as I came in the door.

"I'm back here in the kitchen," she said.

When I entered the kitchen she was running her hands over the granite counter tops and tears were welling up in her eyes. "God, I'm such a baby. I miss him so much, Dev, and I feel like I'm running out on him or something." Then she just broke down and started sobbing. I didn't quite know what to do so I put my arms around her and that seemed to make her cry all the harder.

"Oh, God, look at me, what a mess. If my brothers were here they'd tell me to suck it up. I'm sorry, you shouldn't have to deal with this. It's just me being a little girl."

"No you're not, Casey. You're being a wonderful woman and the best wife ever for loving Dermot so much."

"Yeah, thanks for that, course I was his only wife you know." And then she sort of laughed. She stepped into the bathroom, grabbed some Kleenex, blew her nose then dabbed at her eyes. "There all better. Thanks for picking me up and thanks for not trashing the place while I was gone. Oh, God, I'm gonna miss it," she said and started crying all over again.

"I think it's maybe time for a glass of wine, Casey."

"Do you really think that will help?"

"Well, I'm pretty sure it won't hurt. Besides, we're almost out of time."

She sniffled and looked at me strangely.

"The wine first," I said and pulled a couple of glasses out of the cupboard. I got a corkscrew out of the drawer and opened the bottle, then poured us each a glass.

"Probably should make a toast," I said. "Here's to you and your lovely home."

"Not for long," she said and a tear ran down her cheek which she didn't bother to brush away.

"Hang on, you better take a stool at the counter."

She gave me another strange look.

"Sit down, I'll be back in flash," I said and went into the dining room. I came back carrying the wine box.

"Okay, while you were gone some things have happened," I went on to tell her most of the tale. I glossed over pretty much everything with Fat Freddy, skipped the part about the assault on Dallas, I didn't mention shooting the guy on her staircase or Bulldog breaking in. I did tell her about the secret panel in the cabinet.

"I think this is the reason Dermot was murdered, Casey," I said, then opened the lid on the corrugated wine box to reveal the stacks of twenty dollar bills.

She looked back and forth a half dozen times between me and the currency. "What is this? Where did it come from?"

"It's from some sort of drug caper a few years back, long before you guys bought the place, probably before you even met. It was hidden in the house and a not so nice guy got out of jail and thought he should have it."

"Was he the one?"

"Yes."

"Is he?"

"He won't be a problem. I don't think you have anything to worry about. Including, having to leave. This should take care of that."

"How much, my God, look at it all."

"It's close to five-hundred-grand. I had to use some of it over the course of, well business. Actually, not to rush, but I've been keeping this in a safety deposit box in the bank. I was thinking we'd put it back there for safe keeping and get you access to the box and then you'll be more than covered."

She gave me a questioning look. "You mean I can stay here, keep the house?"

"Yeah, I think Dermot would want that."

She rushed off her stool and had her arms around me, crying harder than the two previous times. "Oh my God, Dev, you are such a wonderful man."

"Casey, that's something I don't hear very often."

"Oh, thank you, thank you, thank you."

Chapter Forty-Nine

It was on the news a few days later. The police had received an anonymous tip about a body along the river. Foul play was suspected, but no further information was available.

Louie was celebrating a court case victory. We were eating cheeseburgers and drinking beer in the office passing the binoculars back and forth while the girls in the apartment across the way took turns standing in front of a window air conditioner. You could see their hair blowing in the blast of cold air.

"God, that is so great. Look at that, they must have that thing set at 'Deep Freeze,'" Louie said.

"Yeah, nice. Hey, do you think it's strange we're celebrating your DUI victory by drinking beer?"

Louie lowered the binoculars and looked at me. "Don't start going all sensitive and thoughtful on me. I like you better as a senseless idiot."

"Just wondering is all."

"Well, don't," he said and went back to leering.

My phone rang. "Haskell Investigations."

"Dev." It was Aaron LaZelle, I braced myself.

"Hi, Aaron, what's up?"

"Thought you might be interested in this, you know the body that was found along the river the other day?"

"A body? Did someone drown?"

He paused for a moment, but didn't comment, then said, "It was Lowell Bulski, the Bulldog."

"Really."

"You don't sound too surprised."

"That guy, not a nice man. You'll have to rent the Twins stadium just to hold all the potential suspects."

"There was something else."

"Which is?" I waited for the boom to drop. Maybe someone saw us there or they found my finger prints or DNA or something.

"We ran ballistics on a weapon that was found with him. We got a match on a number of incidents. One of them was Dermot Gallagher's murder."

"In a way I'm not surprised. Once I found out he owned that house it was almost like the Devil lived there and there was going to be evil happening."

"Was your pal dealing with that crowd?"

"Dermot? No, he was straight as an arrow, a good guy. Maybe Bulldog just wanted the house back or something."

"Umm-hmm," Aaron said, but sounded like he really didn't believe me.

"Any idea what happened to Bulldog?" I asked then held my breath.

"Yeah, someone killed him. Guys like him, we sort of look up and down the street, don't see any likely suspects and its pretty much case closed."

"No loss to the quality of life in town," I said.

"Yeah, he was damaged goods, speaking of which, another friend of yours seems to have moved up in the world."

"Who's that?"

"Freddy Zimmerman, Fat Freddy, rumor is he's taken over Bulldog's spot."

"As enforcer for Tubby?"

"That's what we're hearing?"

"Good luck. It'll be interesting to see how that works."

"Just thought you'd like to know. We released Bulldog's name to the press earlier this afternoon."

"Appreciate the call, Aaron."

"My pleasure and it's your turn to buy dinner next," he said then hung up.

"You need to go down to the station with legal representation?" Louie said as he opened another beer.

"No, just a heads up, it'll be on the news tonight. That body they found along the river the other day, turned out to be Bulldog."

"That jerk, God, good riddance. The city crime rate just dropped by about fifty percent," Louie said then drained a third of his bottle.

We polished off the six-pack. Once the girls across the street got dressed, we lost interest and headed over to The Spot. My phone rang about an hour later. I'd switched her ring tone to a submarine alarm sounding. The thing went off; "Arooooga, arooooga, arooooga." Louie and about a half dozen other folks in the bar looked at me strangely.

"Heidi?" I answered then held my breath and waited for the explosion.

"Dev, I would be *very grateful* and make it worth your while if you would come over right now, I just saw another mouse."

The End

Thanks for taking the time to read <u>Bulldog</u>. If you enjoyed Dev's adventure please tell 2-300 of your closest friends. Don't miss the sample of <u>Double Trouble</u> that follows my shameless self promotion.

Help yourself to my other titles, they're all available on Amazon.

The following titles comprise my list of
'stand alone' works of genius.

Baby Grand
Chow For Now
Slow, Slow, Quick, Quick
Merlot
Finders Keepers
End of the Line
Irish Dukes (Fight Card Series)
written under the pseudonym Jack Tunney.

The following titles comprise the Dev Haskell
series. They can be read in any order;

Russian Roulette: Case 1
Mr. Swirlee: Case 2
Bite Me: Case 3
Bombshell: Case 4
Tutti Frutti: Case 5
Last Shot: Case 6
Ting-A-Ling: Case 7
Crickett: Case 8
Bulldog: Case 9
Double Trouble: Case 10
Twinkle Toes (a Dev Haskell short story)

Visit http://www.mikefaricy.com
Email; mikefaricyauthor@gmail.com
Twitter; @mikefaricybooks
On Facebook; Mike Faricy Books *and* Dev Haskell.

Here's a taste of Double Trouble, the next Dev Haskell novel, enjoy.

Double Trouble

Some years back...

I'd been living life dangerously for the better part of a month. Simultaneously dating the Flaherty sisters, Lissa and Candi, and all the while keeping our three-way relationship a secret from both of them. Their parents were out of town for the night and Candi had returned home supposedly to keep an eye on her younger, fifteen year old brother, Tommy. We'd been doing tequila shots in her parents' basement rec room, and hadn't seen Tommy for hours. I learned later that he'd been hiding in the furnace room.

It was at the very peak of our passionate, tequila-fueled, midnight encounter. Blonde-haired Candi, wearing a hair ribbon and a smile, was on the virtual edge of incredible satisfaction and so, in an effort to encourage, I whispered in her ear, "Oh, Lissa, Lissa, Lissa, you are so good."

Candi suddenly kicked me onto the tiled floor then screamed a number of incoherent expletives. Before I could make up an explanation she staggered into the next room to get her father's hunting rifle. I decided it might be wise to exit so I quickly pulled on my boxers and fled up the basement stairs carrying my jeans.

Other than their initial restraining orders, the threatening emails and then Tommy's video, I hadn't heard from any of the Flahertys in almost a decade....

Chapter One

It was my first day working collections for Andy Lindbergh. Things had slowed in the investigative world so it was maybe a good thing I had the opportunity, maybe, but probably not. Andy had just shut down a sixth month business brainstorm that turned out to be a business brain fart. He had eliminated the middle man, namely funeral parlors, allowing individuals to buy coffins directly from his company, theoretically at a substantial saving.

Two things happened; his existing mortician customers, his bread and butter, became really upset. And, Andy ended up getting stiffed, pardon the pun, intentionally or unintentionally by a number of individuals. He'd shut down the buy-direct operation and had put me on collections in an attempt to minimize losses.

There's something about calling folks for past due payments on coffins that can make for a long day. Not for the first time, I was on the line with a very nice, little old lady who probably still used a rotary dial phone.

"What was that you said?"

"I said I'm calling on behalf of Lindbergh Memorials regarding the past due amount on your account."

The coffin had apparently been for her husband. It wasn't like Andy had the option of digging it up and repossessing the thing so a bit of finesse was needed. Was there even a market for a used coffin? I didn't think so.

"Clarence always dealt with that sort of thing, of course he's passed on," she said making it sound like he was out playing poker with the boys or just running to the hardware store.

"Yes, I'm sure he did, but there is a past due amount on your account and I'd like to work with you to help bring your account current."

"Who did you say was calling?"

Things went downhill from there. At noon I walked into Andy's office, we'd been pals for years.

"How's it going?" he asked and attempted to look hopeful.

"Let me sum it up. I quit."

"Already?"

"Andy, I'm hassling octogenarians on social security regarding their monthly payment that is impossible for them to make. Even if they could hear me, they wouldn't understand what I'm talking about. I don't think I'm cut out for this."

"Maybe you're being too nice."

I placed a stack of files and an Excel spread sheet on his desk.

"You got the wrong guy if you want me to play rough with these folks, I just can't do it."

"You know anyone who could?"

A name immediately popped into my head, but I debated mentioning him. "I know a guy who has dabbled in it a bit, collections that is. I have to be honest and tell you he did time a while back, maybe a year or two ago."

"Is he any good?"

"No, that's why he got caught."

"I meant with the collections."

"Oh, yeah I think he's pretty good, at least as far as I know. Let me check him out and I'll get back to you."

"Thanks for trying, Dev."

"Sorry, Andy, but I'm just not the guy."

Chapter Two

I'd known Tommy Flaherty since before I two timed his older sisters, Candi and Lissa. Even as a young kid Tommy had a reputation for getting into trouble coupled with an inability to realize consequences and an uncanny knack for always being the one who was going to get caught. Not the best of combinations.

He started his crime career early on in the primary grades stealing cafeteria lunch desserts. From there, he jumped to ripping off school lockers in junior high. He moved up to swiping cars in high school. Don't let me forget filming me with at least one of his sisters. Breaking and entering became his passion after senior year, for which he served twenty-four months up in the St. Cloud Reformatory.

Unfortunately, the St. Cloud stint only seemed to serve as a sort of criminal finishing school and upon completing that sentence he graduated to armed robbery, whereupon he was once again arrested and this time served three-and-a-half years in Lino Lakes. At age twenty-four he'd already spent close to a quarter of his life behind bars which wasn't the most sterling point to have on one's résumé. The last I heard, Tommy had drifted into the collections area of the business world in an effort to go straight.

After I fled the basement all those years ago, Candi had phoned her sister Lissa in a drunken rage. The jig was up as the sisters quickly determined I had been dating them simultaneously. They threatened me with castration, filed restraining orders, and then promised further legal action if I ever attempted to contact them again.

I figured after a decade had passed and since I was attempting to help their younger brother I had at least a fighting chance. Well, and then there was the little matter of Tommy's video which I never pursued.

"Hi, Candi please."

"Speaking," she said. I could feel the chill thru the phone.

"Candi, this is Dev Haskell. I...hello. Hello?"

I decided a slightly different tack might work with Lissa.

"Hello."

"Hi, Lissa please don't hang up. I'm trying to reach your brother, Tommy. I have a job opportunity for him, but I don't have a phone number."

"Who the hell is this?"

"Please, don't hang up. It's Dev Haskell."

"Oh hi, Dev. Long time no talk. How are you?"

"Lissa, I'm the dullest guy in town."

"I don't believe that for one minute."

"How have you been, Lissa?"

"Well, my sister's talking to me again, if that's your question."

"Actually, Candi just hung up on me, not more than ten minutes ago. I called her for Tommy's phone number, but as soon as I mentioned my name she hung up."

238

"You really can't blame her, Dev. Calling out my name at a rather intimate moment wasn't the most romantic thing to do, and well, if you'll recall it was all caught on film."

"Yes, and if I recall the three of you made a tidy little profit selling that online."

"You have to admit it was classic. What on earth were you thinking calling her by my name at that most inopportune of moments?"

"That was only because you were so good."

"She was in therapy for a couple of years after dating you."

"Well, you two girls and your little brother selling that video online didn't help matters."

"He's always had a bit of an entrepreneurial streak."

"Hiding in the basement and secretly filming us suggests a sort of warped entrepreneurial perspective, don't you think?"

"Tommy's always been the creative type. Besides, a naked woman swearing at you with a hunting rifle was kind of funny. At least all the YouTube folks seemed to think so."

I thought it best not to go down that road. "Would you happen to have Tommy's phone number?"

"I have to ask why. No offense, but is this something legitimate? Or, is it another sort of half-baked scheme you've cooked up? I hope you're not thinking of revenge, you weren't exactly lily white on that whole deal, Dev. That's really the last thing anyone needs right now, Tommy's been straight for almost a year and Candi's finally been able to get off those meds."

"Actually, that's why I'm calling. I heard he was doing collections. I've got a friend who's looking for someone and I thought of Tommy."

"Is it legitimate?"

"Very, this guy is a straight arrow. You can check him out the company is C. Lindbergh Memorials. My pal is Andy Lindbergh he's the president, third generation. They do headstones, coffins, and just about anything you can think of in that industry. Thing is, there isn't much romance to it, but it could be a source of guaranteed employment for someone like your brother for, well, forever."

"He was doing collections up until recently, student loans. Of course the problem is how are you going to collect from people who don't have any money to begin with? He's been looking for something else so from that standpoint your timing couldn't be better."

"Great, I think he and Andy would really hit it off. Can you give me his number?"

"Why don't you give me yours and I'll have him call you."

"Okay, the sooner the better," I said and gave her my number.

"Great talking, Dev. We should get together, just for old times' sake."

"Yeah, I'd like that, Lissa."

"I'd *really* like it," she said.

__Chapter Three__

Tommy called me the very next day. I'd already forgotten about trying to reach him and was sitting in my office hoping the phone would ring with business. Tommy Flaherty wasn't exactly who I hoped to hear from.

"Haskell Investigations."

"Yeah, I'm looking for the video star that slept with both my sisters." That sort of narrowed it down, but the charge caught me off guard and I had to pause for a half second.

"Dev?"

"Yeah, Tommy?"

"Hey, didn't mean to scare you, man."

"Nice to hear from you, Tommy. How are things going?"

"Well, I've been out of the video biz for quite awhile."

I didn't respond.

"Actually, thanks for asking, things couldn't be better."

In retrospect, from this point forward I don't think anything Tommy told me was true.

"Here's the deal, Tommy, I got a pal who needs help with past due accounts." I went on to give him a brief run down on what, exactly, Andy wanted. Then, I finished up with, "I'll be honest, I tried it and didn't last half a day. I'm just not cut out for collections."

"Most folks aren't, Dev. You've got to really want to help people, not that you don't, but I've been there, between a rock and a hard place. A lot of patience and a little luck can get you on the right track. I'd like to meet your guy, like to see you, too. We should get together, maybe grab a bite sometime."

"Yeah, sure, Tommy, we should do that."

"How about today? Say, maybe one-thirty. You free, man?"

"Free? Today? Well, yeah, I guess, I suppose I can do that. You pick the place, Tommy."

"You know the Over Easy? It's down on East Seventh."

I did know it. It was a twenty-four/seven joint that specialized in a cardiac arrest menu and girls to go. They'd been shut down by the health department for a week at the beginning of summer and there'd been a shooting in the ladies room sometime earlier this month.

"The Over Easy?"

"Yeah, it's just across from Doctor Romance."

Perfect. The sex toy store. You could work up an appetite with battery-operated friends then drift into the Over Easy for a heart-stopping meal.

"One-thirty, yeah, I guess that'll work, looking forward to seeing you again, Tommy."

The Over Easy was actually two old train cars pushed together to form a restaurant. The place was featured in post cards from the 1930s and had pretty much been on a downward slide ever since. I was sitting in a back booth waiting for Tommy, watching the collection of characters and smelling hot griddle grease for the better part of a half hour. The table top and the red vinyl booth seemed to glisten from a patina of cooking oil.

Tommy pulled into a parking place across the street. He was driving a faded red, two-door Datsun sedan with a buckled hood and a tied down trunk. Or, was the dangling bumper tied up to the trunk? It was hard to tell.

He climbed out of the car, stared at the parking meter with the red flag showing time had expired, shook his head, muttered something then crossed the street against traffic carrying what looked like a paper lunch bag.

"Hey, Tommy," some tattooed guy behind the counter called then went back to filling coffee cups.

Tommy responded with a nod as he scanned down the length of booths looking for me.

I waved.

"Dev, nice to see you, man it's been awhile," he said, sliding into the side opposite me. He needed a shave and he looked like he'd slept in his clothes.

"Good to see you, Tommy, been a couple years."

"Yeah, 'spose you heard I had a little vacation, compliments of the system," he said.

I felt like asking "Which time?" instead I just nodded and glanced at the menu. "I appreciate you getting back to me so fast, Tommy. This company, there's no romance to the product line, unless you're maybe a vampire or something."

Tommy looked at me straight faced and didn't blink.

"It's everything you can think of for the funeral biz," I said, then went on to explain Andy's business and what he needed.

"Sounds like just what I'm looking for, stable, with a future. God, my last gig was student loans and I was working on commission. I think I only had a four percent success rate and I was their top guy."

"So here's the contact information," I said, sliding an envelope across the table. Tommy glanced at the envelope then quickly slipped it into his pocket without opening it. I sensed a number of heads watching us and probably coming up with all sorts of weird scenarios.

He dove into breakfast, about five pounds' worth of greasy hash browns, greasy bacon, two greasy fried eggs and something resembling hollandaise sauce slopped over the entire platter. After a few minutes I'd pushed my platter to the side, but Tommy continued to diligently work his way through his.

"You gonna just let all that go to waste?" he said once he finished, then nodded at my heart stopping order.

"Help yourself, if you've got the courage."

Once he cleaned my plate, he sat back and gave a satisfied sort of smile. Maybe a minute or two later he picked up his brown paper lunch bag and said, "Would you excuse me for just a moment." He slid out of the booth and headed for the restroom.

He was gone for a good fifteen minutes. I wasn't surprised. The food at the Over Easy probably had that effect on most people. It was one of the reasons I'd pushed mine to the side. When he returned to the booth, he looked clean shaven.

"Did you just shave in there?"

"Yeah, didn't Lissa mention it? You might say I'm sort of highly mobile, right now."

"Highly mobile?"

"Kind of living in my car, you know, just until I get back on my feet. Shouldn't be too long, well, if this pans out, I hope. And I'm sure it will," he said looking up at me trying to sound positive.

"Your car?" I asked and looked out across the street at the buckled hood and the Bungee Cord holding things together in the rear.

"Couldn't you move in with Candi or Lissa? You know, just till you got back on your feet?"

"That sort of didn't work out too well with either one of them. They thought some things were missing, they never really said anything, but I know they blamed me. I just figured it would probably be better for all of us if I was on my own. Be great to have a place to land, you know for maybe a day or so, couple of days, tops, just to tide me over until I got this job. And I'm gonna get it, I can feel it, Dev."

If I was supposed to respond, I didn't.

"Well, I suppose I should get going. I'll call your pal right away, soon as I find a pay phone. I think there's one a couple of blocks over, maybe."

"You don't have a phone?"

"That's one of the first things I intend to address just as soon as I can. Well, that and I wanted to give some flowers to my Mom. I know, crazy, but it's just something I gotta do. She just loves flowers."

"I thought she passed away a couple of years back?"

"Oh yeah, she did," Tommy said, not meeting my eye. "I just wanted to leave them on her grave, you know make it look nice and all. She was such a wonderful woman."

"Isn't she buried back in Ohio, some sort of family cemetery or something?"

"That's why it's so expensive, I'd have to send them. You know, sort of like Joe DiMaggio did for Marilyn Monroe."

I was beginning to wonder about the wisdom of passing Tommy Flaherty on to Andy.

Tommy picked up the tab and looked at it for a long moment. "You mind if we split this? I just have a C-note and I was hoping I wouldn't have to break it."

"Let me get it, Tommy. My pleasure, besides it was nice to see you again."

"You sure? I mean I can cover my half, if that's what you want to do."

"No, my pleasure. Why don't you give me a call once you talk to Andy? Let me know how things went."

"Yeah, I'd be happy to, Dev. Hey, thanks again, I've sort of been on the short side lately."

"Glad I could help, Tommy, talk to you later."

Chapter Four

Andy phoned me that afternoon. I was just about to head over to The Spot and meet my officemate, Louie, for just one.

"Hey, Andy, how are things?"

"Great, spoke with your guy Flaherty this afternoon."

"Yeah, how'd it go?"

"Sounds like a real nice guy, polite, well-spoken. The last thing I need is some thug making calls. He's coming in tomorrow, but unless he crashes into my car in the parking lot, I'd say he's got the job."

I wasn't sure if I should offer congratulations or a warning. I decided to go positive. "That's great, Andy. I'm sure he'll work out and hopefully ease that list of past dues you're carrying."

"That's my hope, too. Well, just wanted to say thanks."

"No, Andy, thank you for being a good guy and giving him a chance."

"Later," he said and hung up.

I walked over to The Spot. Louie was sitting four stools in from the front door. I signaled Jimmy for a round.

"You're certainly cheery for having accomplished absolutely nothing all day, again," Louie said.

"I'll have you know I did accomplish something today and I'm pretty damn proud of it."

"Do tell," he said then nodded thanks to Jimmy as he slid my beer and Louie's next drink across the bar.

I proceeded to tell him my Tommy tale. How the guy was down and out just fighting for a second chance and coincidently I went the extra mile, was able to get in touch with him and give him Andy's number.

"And, I just got off the phone with Andy. He said he was going to offer Tommy the job."

"Well, you better watch it, much more of this sort of behavior and you'll be confusing all of us who have you pegged as a complete and utter asshole," Louie said then raised his fresh drink to me in a toast.

"Sorry to disappoint," I said.

"We toasted one another for the better part of the evening and I ended up taking the backstreets home. I pulled into my driveway, locked my car and was halfway to the front door when a voice called my name.

"Dev?"

I jumped a couple of feet, looked around, and there was Tommy stepping out of the shadows. "Tommy, God, you scared the hell out of me, what's up?"

"I just wanted to tell you thanks, again. I phoned Andy Lindbergh this afternoon. I think it went pretty well and I have an appointment with him tomorrow. Can't thank you enough for all you've done, man."

"My pleasure, Tommy."

He nodded like that seemed logical then just stood there looking like the new kid in the neighborhood hoping someone would pick him for their team.

I waited for a long, pregnant pause then asked, "You got a place to stay tonight?"

248

"My car, I was gonna park on one of the side streets down by the police station. It's pretty safe down there, most of the time, usually."

"Look, I got a spare couch. Why don't you come on in and get a decent night's sleep, shower and shave tomorrow morning so you're on your best foot going in to talk with Andy."

"That's awfully nice of you, Dev. You sure I wouldn't be cramping your style?"

"Tommy, it's after two in the morning and I didn't bring anyone home. I don't have a lot going on right now so grab your stuff and come on in."

"I'm traveling light," he said and followed me up the steps.

I showed him where the guest bath was and got him a glass of water. "If you're the first one up tomorrow this is how you make the coffee," I said pouring water into the coffee maker then scooping six spoonfuls of grounds into the filter. "See that button at the base of the coffee pot?"

"Yeah."

"All you gotta do is push that thing."

"I think I can remember that."

"What time are you meeting Andy tomorrow?"

"Eleven, I'm praying I'll be walking out of there with a job."

"Just be yourself, Tommy. Who wouldn't want to hire you?"

Chapter Five

Tommy was gone by the time I got up, but then again it was almost noon. The coffee was still on with maybe a half-cup left in the pot. I just hoped all went well for both him and more importantly, Andy.

"Just calling to say thanks, again," Andy said when he called a little after four.

"You hired him?"

"Yeah, in fact right now he's working at the same desk where you failed so miserably, he's been making collection calls since noon. No offense, but he's already done about a thousand percent better than you."

"Terrific."

"Yeah, he wanted to work until eight tonight, said you actually get the best results between six and eight. Which I guess sort of makes sense."

"He'd know better than me."

"Or me. Anyway, I just wanted to thank you again, Dev. He's gonna be a great addition. I'm thinking there are all sorts of possibilities for someone with his talents."

"Glad to hear it, Andy, and thanks for giving him a chance."

"Your guy get the job?" Louie asked looking up from the picnic table that served as his desk.

"Not only did he get it, but he's working there right now. Andy says he's already making an impact and wants to work until about eight tonight, says between six and eight is the best time to connect with folks for collections. Andy's thrilled."

"Great, so it's a win all around?"

"Yeah, you know every once in a while I guess you can do something nice for someone and it doesn't come back and bite you in the ass."

We wandered over to The Spot for a few hours to celebrate Tommy's success. When I pulled into my driveway later that night Tommy was standing on the front porch. It looked like he was just knocking on the door.

"So?" I said climbing the front steps.

"Oh hi, Dev, didn't realize you weren't home. Hey, I got the job. Actually, I worked until eight tonight, really a nice guy."

"Well, I gotta tell you, I got a call from him this afternoon and he's pretty damn happy. You'll be a great addition there, Tommy."

"I can't thank you enough for the help, all the advice, putting me in touch with Andy and of course the place to stay last night."

"My pleasure, Tommy. What are your plans for tonight?"

"Tonight?"

"That pretty much answers my question, you want to flake out on my couch again?"

"Would you mind? I have to be at work tomorrow by ten. God, it feels great having a job to go to."

"Come on in," I said then slipped my key in the lock. My front door was unlocked and I figured I must

251

have forgotten to lock the door on my way out that morning which was very unusual for me.

I was going to throw some cold pizza in the microwave, but there wasn't any in the fridge so I ordered another. Tommy had a piece when it arrived, but didn't seem that hungry. He flaked out on the couch while I had another beer. I was going to make coffee for the morning, but it was already made. I figured I was losing my mind if I couldn't remember making it and the best thing to do was just go to bed.

I spent the following day checking references and employment details on about a hundred job applications for a client, then I called Heidi to see about a night of debauchery.

"Hi, Heidi, you got any plans for tonight?"

"Nothing that can't be postponed if the right offer comes across."

"I would be happy to bring dinner over, or if you feel like it, I could wine and dine you at some intimate little place."

"What's this going to cost me?"

"Cost you? Nothing. You won't have to pay a cent."

"I wasn't talking money, Dev."

"Well, I don't know, I suppose we could sort of see how the night goes and maybe…."

"I was kidding, dopey. It's just nice to hear you grovel."

"If it wasn't so good, I wouldn't have made this call in the first place, believe me you're good and I'm groveling."

"Pick me up at seven and you choose the place, but please, let's go somewhere nice this time. Not those usual greasy spoon dives you go to for cheeseburgers and beer. Pick someplace romantic."

"We could do dinner in bed."

"I'll see you at seven and don't be late."

I was at Heidi's at 7:15, she wasn't ready. We ended up at a quiet little Italian restaurant over on University forty minutes later. Despite the sheet of plywood covering the broken glass in the front door, it had the feel of a family place and apparently tonight the family wasn't talking. The wife served as hostess and her husband was our waiter. They were both pleasant enough when dealing with us, but when they were away from the table we could hear them arguing in the kitchen.

"I wonder what he did," Heidi said.

"I heard it on the news the other night, someone stole their ATM machine, hauled it right out of the place. That's why there's plywood over the front door."

"Then I don't blame her for being unhappy," Heidi said and sipped.

I weighed my options, thought about the potential for the rest of the night. "You're absolutely right."

She looked at me for a long moment and said, "That was sweet, Dev."

Despite the bickering emanating from the restaurant kitchen, we had a pleasant meal. On the way home, Heidi had that warm glow she gets when she's very content and has been a little overserved. "Want to come in for a glass of wine and stay for breakfast?" she asked as we pulled up in front of her place.

"I think that sounds like a great idea." I spent the night and woke up just long enough to hear Heidi tell me thanks before she flew out the door, then I rolled over and drifted back to sleep.

I went home to shower and change. Something didn't seem right the moment I stepped in the door. I couldn't quite put my finger on it and then I realized I smelled coffee. The pot was empty, the kitchen looked like I'd left it, but I was sure I smelled coffee. I felt the pot, it wasn't warm, or was it? I opened the top and there wasn't a filter or grounds in there, but there was moisture. I wasn't sure, maybe it was just from the day before.

I checked the dishwasher, there were more mugs than usual, but then again Tommy had spent two nights here so that sort of made sense. Was the shower wet? I'd already turned it on when I noticed water on the glass, maybe, I couldn't really tell. I wondered if I was becoming paranoid.

I had to deliver my results on all the employment references to my client later in the afternoon and I wanted to wear something more than a T-shirt. I pulled on some decent slacks, a clean golf shirt, but couldn't find the sport coat I was looking for and wondered if I'd left it at someone's house. Once again, the thought of losing what was left of my mind bounced around in my thick skull.

Chapter Six

A couple of days later I was at my desk scanning the apartment building across the street through my binoculars. One of the girls in the third floor unit had been running back and forth from the kitchen to a bedroom wearing just a towel around her head. I sat waiting patiently for her next appearance when the phone rang.

"Haskell Investigations," I said holding the phone with my left hand and the binoculars with my right.

"Dev, Heidi."

"Everything all right?"

"Yeah, I'm looking for a date, you busy tonight?"

"I'm sure I'll be able to deliver whatever particular perversion you're in the mood for."

"Not what I meant, you perv. I have to go to a fundraiser tonight, a client sent me tickets. I just need someone on my arm. I had one of my girlfriends lined up, but she canceled."

"Let me guess, that Mary Francis person."

"How did you know?"

"Because she always cancels. Yeah, I can go with you. What time do you want me to pick you up?"

"Is six okay?"

"I'll be there," I said and went back to scanning across the street.

Heidi's fundraising events were quasi-formal things that collected a higher class of criminal than the ones I usually rubbed shoulders with. These were big-time scammers; lawyers, politicians, bankers and business owners. The hors d'oeuvres would be lousy and too few, with lite beer that was warm and overpriced, watered-down drinks that were too expensive. Heidi usually made it worth my while at the end of the night.

I rang her doorbell right on time, after the third ring Heidi answered the door in her bathrobe.

"Don't say anything. I'm almost ready, just give me a moment. Go pour yourself a beer in the kitchen."

I did as commanded, then sat on a kitchen stool and sipped.

"Just be a minute," she called about fifteen minutes later. I'd been here before, many times before. I figured since the hors d'oeuvres were bound to be lousy I'd search her cupboards. I came up with rice cakes and an opened bag of lime-flavored Dorito chips that were so stale they didn't crunch when I bit into one. I ate them anyway.

"Almost ready," she said after maybe another five minutes. The chips were gone and the beer was empty, I debated opening another.

"Just going to pee and then we'll go," she called sometime after that. I should have opened that second beer ten minutes earlier. I heard the toilet flush, then the sink running, then something spray or spritz. She walked into the kitchen and looked at me while she attached an earring. "That's what you're wearing?"

"I suppose I could run home and change."

She actually seemed to think about that option for a moment then said, "No, we're already late. Do you have a tie in the car?"

"I'm not wearing a tie."

She shook her head then picked up a purse and keys. The purse was small, a little sort of fancy white beaded thing. It looked like it would barely hold a couple of credit cards and I wondered how that was going to work.

"Here, just carry these for me," she said then handed me a comb, a hair brush with a folding handle, lipstick, an eyebrow pencil, some sort of makeup compact thing, and a small perfume bottle.

"What do you want me to do with all this?"

"Just bring it and don't complain," she said.

I headed to the car as she locked the front door.

"We better take my car. No telling what people would think if we arrived in that bomb of yours."

I was driving a silver Sebring, no whitewalls, with a trunk that was sprayed flat black. I'd gotten a great deal on it at the police auction.

"You want me to drive your car?"

"Yeah, I've got some touch up to do," she said then stood next to the passenger door of her BMW and waited for me to open it for her. I watched her get in, then dumped all the things I was supposed to carry in her lap and closed the door.

She had the mirror on the sun visor down before I climbed behind the wheel.

"Heidi, you look wonderful, you always do, just relax and enjoy the ride."

"Just a little touch," she said doing something to her eye with a pencil. "Where'd you get that coat?" she asked referring to my black and white checked sport coat.

"Like it?"

"Not really."

"I got it at Sonny's."

"The bargain rack? I'm amazed they even let you out of the store with that thing."

"I think it looks great."

"The collar tab on your shirt is unbuttoned."

"Yeah, the button must have come off at the dry cleaners."

"Or, when it was lying on your bedroom floor for a week."

"Are we going to be happy by the time we get there?"

"Okay, here's the deal, I think a potential client is going to be here and maybe I'm just a little nervous. I've been working on this guy for over a year."

"A little nervous, you've been bitching since you let me in the door. Anything I can do to help?"

"Yes, escort me in the door then stay away. I'll signal if I need anything."

"Sounds fun."

"It's business for me, Dev. You'll get your reward at the end of the night, provided you behave."

"I promise to be good," I said.

Chapter Seven

I was lying awake on the couch at Casey's wondering why Bulldog wanted to get into this place. It's not like there was anything to really steal, maybe the flat screen, but a jerk like Bulldog would have access to an entire truckload just by making a phone call. Dermot's laptop was three or four years old and besides, I didn't think Bulldog knew the alphabet. Then there was the bit that he, Bulldog was a previous owner. Knowing Dermot and Casey, they would have run the other way rather than deal with someone like him. I double checked to make sure the .38 was on the coffee table then promised myself I'd call Casey in the morning and drifted off to sleep.

"Rise and shine, Sleeping Beauty," Casey called and set down a couple of bags and a tray holding four coffees.

I sort of groaned then rolled over and sat up. My shoulders, neck and back made audible cracking sounds as I twisted left and right, then I burped.

"Charming. God, you slob, how could you trash this place all by yourself in just one night?" she asked then placed my ice cream dish in the bowl full of chicken wing bones. She stacked the empty dip container on top and picked it all up along with the cracker box. "I'll come back and get all the beer bottles and I better bring the vacuum, you've got crumbs all over. There are toothbrushes in the top drawer to the right of the bathroom sink. Might be a good idea, then come on back, if I remember correctly you like caramel rolls for breakfast."

"I like anything I don't have to cook," I said. Then picked up the .38 as discreetly as possible and slipped it into my pocket.

We were sitting in the den. Two plumbers were banging pipes out in the front room doing something to the radiator. I was almost finished with my second coffee and eyeing the third. Casey was nibbling at the same caramel roll she'd started twenty minutes earlier. She was doing the female thing; taking the smallest of bites, barely a morsel, eating that and then waiting. I'd already inhaled both my caramel rolls and was picking up errant crumbs from off the coffee table. I eyed the rest of her's and decided to play rough.

"God, I guess I should have gotten more," she said watching me lick my finger tips.

"Nah, this was great. Really hits the spot. I have to say, Casey, you look really great, have you lost a little weight?"

"Probably just the stress."

"Well, you look like you've been working out."

"Thanks, Dev, that's sweet," she said then pushed her plate to the center of the coffee table. "Go ahead and finish that if you want, I'm really not that hungry."

"Nah, I couldn't."

"Please, take it otherwise it will just go to waste."

"Okay, I guess if you really don't want it."

"No really, I'm full."

"Hey, mind if I ask you something?" I said then took a bite that cut her caramel roll in half.

"Ask me and we'll see."

"How long have you guys been in this house?"

"You mean like why isn't it finished?"

"No, I didn't mean it like that."

There was a sort of window bay area maybe five feet deep on the exterior wall of the den with four tall windows. The roof had leaked and probably still did. Casey glanced up at the water-damaged plaster on the ceiling. It was cracked and stained a yellow brownish color. Unfortunate past experience told me those stains would bleed right through any paint.

"All our friends from the burbs always asked us when we were going to be finished. They just didn't get it. Anyway, let's see, it was May when we moved in, and we had to get the furnace replaced before we moved. I think we closed the end of March. So that's..." She counted silently on her fingers, then said, "So I guess that's about twenty-eight months."

"You remember who you bought it from?"

She ignored my question and took a detour down memory lane instead. "It was going to be our house forever. I mean with four bedrooms upstairs there'd be plenty of room for kids. We were going to live here for the next fifty years. Of course things happen and..."

"You remember who you bought it from?"

"I can't really say. It was sort of strange. It was never officially on the market. We sort of heard about it by word of mouth, I can't even remember who told us. Sort of a weirdo character at the closing representing the sellers. A lawyer I think, Johnny or Jamie something. I suppose I've got his card around here somewhere in a file, sleazy type, with a home dye-job on dreadful slicked back hair. He kept leering and when he gave me his card he sort of held my hand and raised his eyebrows like there was a lot more available."

"What did you do?"

"Ran to the ladies room and washed my hands with disinfectant, twice. What a creep. We never met the owners, I think they were traveling or something?"

"Traveling, like they were in the circus or what?"

"Yeah, that's right, Dev, the circus."

"Hey, how would you feel if I moved in, temporarily, just so the place isn't empty at night?"

"Did you see him, did he come back?"

"No, nothing like that," I lied.

"Hey, I appreciate the offer, Dev, but I really can't impose on you."

"Casey, it wouldn't be an imposition. Really, besides you'll sleep better so how 'bout we just agree I'll spend the nights here."

"I could pay you, not much, but…"

"No. You don't need to pay me. I'd like to do it."

"You're sure?"

"Yup."

"I mean I could probably…."

"No, Casey, look I'll be back here around five tonight. If you could go out today, maybe get me a set of keys, we'll be all set."

"I suppose you could use Dermot's," she said and then the tears welled up again.

Dev's about to get pushed into the deep end. You can lend a helping hand by getting a copy of Double Trouble. Many thanks, and enjoy the read, Mike Faricy